Vlad V (Book 4)

Vampires of Transylvania

By Mit Sandru

Chivileri Publishing

Copyright © 2014 by Dumitru Sandru

ISBN-13: 978-1-942612-02-5

Table of Contents

CHAPTER 1 7
CHAPTER 2 13
CHAPTER 3 21
CHAPTER 4 27
CHAPTER 5 37
CHAPTER 6 45
CHAPTER 7 51
CHAPTER 8 59
CHAPTER 9 63
CHAPTER 10 69
CHAPTER 11 75
CHAPTER 12 81
CHAPTER 13 87
CHAPTER 14 91
CHAPTER 15 97
CHAPTER 16 103
CHAPTER 17 107
CHAPTER 18 113
CHAPTER 19 119
CHAPTER 20 125
CHAPTER 21 129
CHAPTER 22 135
CHAPTER 23 141
CHAPTER 24 147
CHAPTER 25 153
CHAPTER 26 157
CHAPTER 27 161
CHAPTER 28 167
CHAPTER 29 171

The previous book in this series is
"Vampire Slayers" (Vlad V Book 3)

Vlad V the vampire warned Cat that when you're rich, the stakes are much higher, and that she might have to do appalling things to survive. Cat thought she'd have to deal with unscrupulous lawyers, greedy financiers and bankers, Wall Street shysters, corrupt politicians, devious conmen, and depraved socialites. Instead, an old nemesis allied with a vampire-slayer drug cult came out of the dark, demanding extortion money or she would be killed. Capturing a vampire—Vlad V perhaps—would be an added bonus for the cult. Blue vampire blood could provide perpetual life and additional riches. Unfortunately, the villains don't know who or what they are dealing with. Never upset the great-granddaughter of Vlad V and Angelique, her vampire friend, if you want to stay healthy and alive.

Chapter 1

Buffeted by turbulent weather the Learjet jerked and rolled, bumped and dropped. The captain turned the seatbelt light on, and I fastened mine. Outside, mean black clouds roiled around us. A big storm was engulfing Europe, from England to Romania and beyond. Would there be a clear sky with a full moon in a couple of nights, when I'd have to spread Vlad's ashes in Transylvania? Was I supposed to spread the ashes from the Clock Tower in Sighisoara only during a clear full moon? Or maybe it didn't matter, as long as I emptied Vlad's ashes precisely at midnight. Considering the weather conditions in this part of the world, I couldn't imagine many clear night skies. I decided to worry about this detail when I'd be at the top of the tower at midnight on that night.

The captain came toward me. "Miss Cat, we are experiencing rough weather from here to our destination."

"A rocky ride," I replied, with a faint smile.

"I have some bad news. The airport in Sibiu is flooded from the storm. We cannot land there. We could land in Munich and wait until the bad weather passes farther to the east."

"I must be in Sighisoara two days from now. Can you land in Timisoara?" As I recalled, that city had an international airport as well.

"I'll have to check. But how would you get to your destination from Timisoara?"

"I'll arrange ground transportation," I said.

"Very well, let me check." He went back into the cockpit.

The stewardess came over with an opened bottle of champagne to refill my glass, but I raised my hand to stop her. I needed a clear head as we approached Transylvania, the land of vampires.

I was traveling alone. My vampire friends, Angelique and François, had remained behind in New York. Angelique was still suffering from the gunshots and from the White Fog drug that Cadogan, the vampire slayers' cult leader, had given in her. François was a doctor, besides being a vampire, and had stayed with Angelique to treat her. The bullets inside her were not the problem, according to François; it was the reaction of the lead and the drug producing a poison that affected Angelique. Very few things can cause illness in vampires, and even fewer can kill them. But this time Angelique wasn't so lucky. François was sure, though, that with proper care she would make a full recovery.

The captain returned. "Good news, Miss Cat. We can land at Traian Vuia International Airport in Timisoara. The weather is better there than in the heart of Transylvania."

"Excellent, let's do that."

Smiling, the captain raised two fingers to his temple in salute and went back to plan for our new destination.

I called my travel agent back in New York to reserve ground transportation. Then I called Mundibuto, my other vampire friend. He was possibly the only black vampire in the world. He had offered me his help and so would join me in Sighisoara, traveling from Nigeria. He was an American who found Africa more favorable to his style of living. My great-great-great grandfather Vlad V Draculesti had saved him from a lynching 200 years ago in South Carolina and had set him free. Mundibuto then became a sailor and was infected with the Egyptian vampire strain. Vlad V came to his aid and helped him become a vampire. Vampires are not dead—they're very much alive, and they have blue blood.

Mundibuto was already in Bucharest, waiting to hear from me. I told him about my change of plans and that we would make contact in Sighisoara.

The rest of the flight continued to be bumpy, but we landed safely at Timisoara's airport. The weather outside was cloudy and the tarmac was wet, but there was no rain falling. The captain taxied the plane off to the side of the terminal, where a limo and a customs van were waiting for us. The plane finally stopped, and the stairway was lowered. Two Romanian customs officials, a man and a woman, boarded the plane. Traveling by Learjet has its benefits—VIP treatment. The woman inspected my passport.

"Business or pleasure?" she asked, smiling.

"Pleasure. I came to visit Transylvania," I answered.

She stamped my passport. "Ahh! Too bad you were forced to land on the western fringes of Transylvania. Hopefully, the weather will improve. Enjoy Romania, and welcome to Timisoara."

The two customs agents smiled, saluted, and deplaned to return to the terminal.

I picked up my backpack bag, said good-bye to the crew, and descended to the tarmac, where the limo was waiting for me. Arrangements were made for me to stay the night at the Hotel Continental and then depart from Timisoara to Sighisoara the next morning by car. After my one piece of luggage was loaded into the trunk, the limo took off toward the city center.

"Welcome to Timisoara," said the driver. "My name is Dorin Ionescu, at your service. Please call me Dorin."

"Hi, Dorin. I'm Cat Sanders. You speak English well. I believe you're taking me to the Hotel Continental."

"Certainly. Nice to make your acquaintance, and thank you—speaking several languages is part of my post."

Make my acquaintance? Such formal English. I smiled. "You may call me Cat, as in Catherina."

"Certainly. May I ask what brings you to our beautiful city?"

"Actually, I came to see Transylvania."

"That is correct. The travel agency reserved me to drive you there. I will be your driver for your entire stay here in Romania."

"Well, great."

"Should you wish to go anywhere tonight, just give me a call and I will take you there."

I still wasn't used to being a billionaire. For a moment I thought, *how much will this cost me?* But then, why worry? I can afford a private chauffeur. I picked up one of his cards and looked at it. *Dorin Ionescu, Private Chauffeur and Guide.* "Sure thing."

"And tomorrow Stanca, my wife, will be our escort."

"Escort? You mean tour guide?"

"Yes, yes. Tour guide. We were told that you'd appreciate a good tour of Transylvania."

"Yes, the land of the vampires," I said.

He smiled knowingly in the rearview mirror. "Vampires. Certainly."

"I need to be in Sighisoara two days from now. Can it be done?"

Dorin bobbed his head. "Certainly. We will be there by tomorrow evening."

We left behind fields and industrial buildings, and entered the city. Timisoara was a quaint provincial town with an Austrian architectural style. Trees and parks were abundant. Tramways crisscrossed our path, taking the locals to and fro.

We crossed a steep riverbank, and Dorin said, "That is Bega, our river. Actually, it is a canal connecting to the Danube. It was built a long time ago to drain the swamps and for river commerce."

Several sweep-oar boats were cruising on the river-canal as if in training. "Do you have a university in this city?" I was curious about the boats.

"Yes, we have a big university here—several schools of medicine, agriculture, engineering, and sciences, and many others. I am not an educated man myself, so I cannot recall all the schools at the University of Timisoara."

"How many inhabitants are in your city?"

11

"About 300,000 people. The city is over 800 years old," answered Dorin. "That is the Romanian Orthodox Metropolitan Cathedral." We drove by a large church of an unusual architecture—very geometric and very tall. The roofs of the many towers was made of green glazed tiles and decorated with artistic designs made of yellow and red tiles.

As we approached a grand plaza, he pointed to a marble-clad building. "That is the Opera House."

They have an opera house here in this small city? And then something caught my eye—an individual in a black raincoat was walking toward the doors of the Opera House. "Stop the car, please!" I demanded.

Startled, Dorin pulled over. I jumped out of the limo and ran toward the figure walking ahead of me. It couldn't be who I thought it was, but from the back the resemblance to Vlad was uncanny. I knew it was just a coincidence, but I wished to see this man's face. I picked up my pace, as fast as I could walk in my platform sandals, to catch up with him. Dorin followed me. The man opened one of the heavy, black wooden doors and went inside. I followed quickly after him.

Chapter 2

I stepped inside the Opera House. For a moment, I felt lost in its opulent marble and gilded foyer, done in the typical style of all European opera houses. Two large marble spiral staircases led to the upper floors. The stranger, resembling Vlad from the back, could not have gone up there. He must have walked to the orchestral main hall through the red velvet curtain ahead of me. I pushed the curtains aside and found myself in a beautiful, well-lit theatre with red velvet seats and gold gilded balconies. A giant crystal chandelier hung from the golden ceiling.

There was no one in there. The stranger had vanished. Even up in the balconies, there was no one. Did he come in here at all? Soft steps approached from behind, and I turned, expecting to see my driver.

Instead, a blond man in a white tuxedo and red bow tie came toward me. "How may I help you?" The man spoke English to me as if he already knew that I was an American.

"I was wondering if you've seen a man in a black trench coat come in here."

He shook his head. "No. Only you. And him." He pointed to Dorin, who was standing by the red velvet curtains.

Dorin came toward me and said something to him in Romanian, from which I understood the word "tourist." The blond man smiled and swept his hand at the richly decorated interior. "You like?"

"Gorgeous! You people must like opera a lot."

They both nodded and smiled at me.

I must have looked like some disoriented sightseer. Since there were only the three of us there, I had to end my brief visit of the Opera House. "*Multumesc,*" I thanked him in Romanian with a word I had learned during my time on the plane.

"*Cu placere.* My pleasure," he answered. "And please, come by again to see a performance."

I smiled, took another look at the beautiful interior, and left with Dorin. A couple of minutes later we arrived at the Hotel Continental, and soon after I was in my room on the tenth floor.

My right cheek felt hot and throbbing. A few days ago, Melantha, the Goth "princess" and follower of Cadogan, had backslapped me, and her diamond ring had cut my cheek. I should have gone to see my doctor, but I was too busy, so I treated it myself instead. But the wound was now infected, and I needed a doctor.

I called my chauffeur. "Hello, Dorin. I need some medical attention. Can you take me to a clinic, please?"

"Certainly, Cat. I'll be waiting for you at the hotel entrance."

Dorin took me to a small clinic not far from the hotel, and he assisted me in getting the necessary help, including filling out the required forms.

Dressed in a white lab coat, a young doctor—in his thirties, with black hair and gorgeous emerald-green eyes—came over to attend to me. "Hello,

14

Miss Catherina Sanders?" He checked my name on the form I had filled out earlier. "I'm Dr. Lupu."

"Hello."

He extended his hand and I took it. I felt reassured; his hand was soft and warm, and he applied just the right amount of pressure while shaking my hand. "What seems to be the problem, Miss?" And he, too, spoke English well.

"This wound on my cheek is hurting me." I pointed to my bandage.

"Let's have a look. Would you come this way?"

I followed him into a small room, where he invited me to sit on the customary paper-lined, brown vinyl clinic bed. He pulled an overhead light closer, put his latex gloves on, and gently removed the adhesive bandage.

"How did you get this cut, Miss Sanders?" he asked, inspecting my wound.

"Some woman slapped me and cut me with her diamond ring."

"That's terrible. A jealous woman?" He smiled.

"No, just a mad woman." I didn't tell him that a few minutes after she slapped me, Angelique, my vampire friend, ripped her head off. But there was no need to dwell on tragic events.

"The wound is slightly infected. I just need to clean it and apply some medicated ointment. I will use adhesive stitches to close the tear in your skin. Does this hurt?" He touched my wound and I winced. "I'll inject a little bit of painkiller, Novocain, to numb your cheek. This will hurt just a bit."

A nurse came by with a tray, and he picked up a syringe from it. In contrast to the doctor being so gentle and nice, the nurse gave me a cold stare. He didn't have a wedding ring on his finger, so maybe she saw me as a possible threat for Dr. Lupu's heart? I felt the prick of the needle, but I acted bravely. In an instant my cheek felt chilled and numb. Dr. Lupu started cleaning my wound, while another nurse came in to assist the good-looking doctor. She assessed me apprehensively. I wondered what kind of threat I would pose to them, unless they knew him better and his demeanor showed his interest in me. Did they observe the sparkle in my eyes when I looked at him? Who knows, I might have been his type, and perhaps he was showing more than a casual interest in me. Maybe he liked blondes.

He finished and applied an adhesive bandage over my wound. "You're as good as new. You'll have a scar, and when you return to America, you may want to see a plastic surgeon." He smiled at me. "Your face is too pretty to be blemished."

"Thank you, Doctor." I was pleased by his remark.

"Call me Tudor," he said warmly.

"Call me Cat."

The two nurses were hovering nearby, giving me murderous glares. "Would you like to have a cup of coffee with me?" He extended his hand toward the corridor, where I saw his office was located. I observed one of the nurses rolling her eyes.

"Sure, why not? Thanks." And I followed him.

"What would you like? Regular coffee, espresso, or a cappuccino?" He invited me to sit in one of his leather chairs.

"A cappuccino would be great." I sat down and admired his many diplomas hanging on the walls.

"*Doua cappuccinos, te rog*," he instructed his plump, middle-aged secretary outside his office. He sat across from me on the other chair.

"I hope I'm not disturbing your busy schedule," I said.

"We're not that busy at the moment. You were our only patient at this hour."

I touched my bandage. I didn't feel any pain. "Your English sounds like American English. Where did you learn it?"

"I studied English in school, and I spent a few years in New York City. There was a program made available to young Romanian doctors to practice in the West. And I was the lucky one to be selected. What brings you to Romania, to Timisoara?"

"Oh, my plane had to land here because of the storms, but I was on my way to Sighisoara, to visit the land of Dracula." I made my eyes big with excitement.

He laughed heartily. "You people in the West are so fascinated with Dracula and vampires." His secretary brought in our cappuccinos.

"It's true. Maybe because it is appealing to live forever."

"You know, vampires bite you and suck your blood, and then you become one of them, one of the living dead," he said, smiling.

"Here in Transylvania, you must have seen, on occasion, a vampire or two."

"Well, we are in the greater area of Transylvania. Timisoara is located in a region called Banat.

Transylvania proper, and the hotbed of vampires, is to the east. And although I've seen and even treated a few bloodsuckers, I have never had the privilege of encountering a true vampire."

I giggled and took a sip of my cappuccino. It was good. Outside his office, one of the nurses was inquiring about something. Tudor leaned toward the door and said, "*Sint ocupat.*" He turned to me and said, "I told them I'm busy."

"Dr. Tudor—"

"Just Tudor," he replied with a smile.

"Tudor, thank you for your hospitality, but I must be going. Tomorrow I leave for Sighisoara."

"How are you getting there, Cat?"

"By car. I've made arrangements."

"Very well. It was a pleasure to have met you, Cat, and to be of assistance. I hope you'll stop and visit me on your way back."

I stood up and shook his hand, and then a thought crossed my mind. "Have you ever heard of a certain Dr. Hellinherr, an Austrian? A long time ago, he lived here in your city."

"Hellinherr?" While holding my hand, he thought for a second. "No, I'm afraid not."

"Well, it was just a thought I had," I said, still holding his hand. It felt pleasant, feeling his manly energy.

"However, I have an old doctor friend, my mentor, Dr. Valo Predescu, who might know about your Dr. Hellinherr. Let me give him a call. Please have a seat while I call him."

I let go of his hand and sat down. He pulled his cellphone from his coat pocket and speed-dialed a number. It seemed that his friend answered, and they engaged in a discussion. I could understand him inquiring about Dr. Hellinherr and referring to me as *Americana*, and then Tudor listened intently for a minute.

He pressed the phone to his chest and said, "What do you know! Dr. Valo knows of a Dr. Hellinherr from before and during the war. World War II, that is."

I was surprised at first that someone still remembered him. So it was true, what Vlad had told me about Dr. Hellinherr Sr. or Jr.—I wasn't sure which one—having a laboratory in the city of Timisoara. "What do you know?" I commented.

"Would you like to talk to him?"

"Yes."

Tudor spoke a few words and then handed me his phone. "Hello," I said. "This is Cat Sanders. Dr. Tudor tells me that you know Dr. Hellinherr."

"Hello," answered an old man. "This is Dr. Valo Predescu. I'm pleased to know you, even if it is only by phone. Yes, I knew a Dr. Hellinherr, but that was a long time ago."

"I wonder if you know where he worked, where his laboratory was."

"Where he worked," repeated Dr. Valo. "Well, he was also a professor of medicine at the university. As far as his laboratory, he had several. But I tell you what—why don't you come and visit us, and we can chat some more. Perhaps you can join my wife and me for dinner, along with Dr. Tudor?"

That surprised me. I had heard that Romanians were friendly, but I didn't expect to be invited for dinner. Or maybe Tudor had asked him to act as a matchmaker?

Chapter 3

Was Tudor interested in me? He was good-looking and a doctor. It pleased me that he found me attractive. No wonder the nurses at the clinic were giving me the evil eye! This would give me a chance to get to know him better, and I wanted to question Dr. Valo about Dr. Hellinherr. "Sure, thank you Dr. Predescu. I'll let you speak to Tudor." I gave the phone back to him.

Tudor spoke briefly and then ended the call with a big smile. "Well, I had intended to ask you out to dinner this evening, but Dr. Valo made a date for all of us." He looked happy.

I smiled knowingly. "In that case, I'd better return to my hotel, and maybe later you can pick me up for dinner. I'm staying at the Hotel Continental."

"Absolutely. I'll pick you up at six? They eat early," he said, referring to the Predescus.

"That's fine. I'll see you then." I shook his hand and he escorted me to the lobby, to the relief of the two nurses. Dorin was waiting for me to take me back to the hotel.

Historically, Dr. Hellinherr Sr. and his family were François, Angelique, and Vlad's menace, and perhaps a menace to all vampires. The Austrian doctor had sought vampires and their blood to create a superhuman race. His descendant, Dr. Hellinherr III, back in the US, was pursuing the same agenda and, on two occasions, he had almost gotten his hands on Vlad and Angelique. He didn't scare me, except for what he could do if he were to

21

get vampire blue blood. Besides, I was not a vampire, although my lineage went back to Vlad V Draculesti—the nephew of Vlad III, the Impaler, also known as Dracula.

At six o'clock, Tudor called me from the lobby and I went down to meet him. He had a bouquet of lavender roses and a box of chocolates for me.

He saw the surprise on my face. "In Romania, it is customary to bring flowers and chocolates to a beautiful woman like you."

"How sweet!" I was indeed surprised by his gesture. And he had brought me lavender roses, a symbol of enchantment and love at first sight. I took the flowers and chocolates and joined him in his Beamer. On the back seat, he had a bouquet of assorted carnations, another box of chocolates, and a bottle of Scotch for the Predescus.

We arrived shortly at Dr. Valo's house, right across the river-canal Bega. Dr. Valo met us at the door. He was an elderly, distinguished-looking man with combed-back silver hair and blue eyes. We shook hands and then he kissed my hand, like an old-fashion European gentleman. I'd have to say that I liked it. Inside, I met his wife, Voichita, a very nice lady with exquisite manners. After all the formalities were done, including the proffering of the gifts Tudor had brought, we sat down at a table on a terrace overlooking the backyard, which had a garden and an orchard with many fruit trees.

Of course, I told them what had brought me to their city: my desire to see Transylvania. We made small talk while sipping champagne and eating the delicious hors d'oeuvres that Voichita had made.

"So—Dr. Hellinherr," said Dr. Valo. "Why do you want to know about them? They weren't particularly nice people."

"Which of the Hellinherrs are you referring to?" I asked.

"Both of them. The senior and the junior, although I knew the junior," replied Dr. Valo. "I was a medical student during the war and knew Dr. Hellinherr Jr. two years before he left in '46 to go to America. My father, a very good doctor, and I were surprised that he immigrated to America after what he had done."

"What did he do?" I asked.

"They had experimented on people before and during the war. That's what my father told me, in confidence. They had a laboratory near the Nord Trainstation, and prisoners from the concentration camps, mostly Jews, were delivered to their laboratory through secret tunnels."

"Was that for the senior or the junior's experiments?"

"Both of them."

"But I thought the senior died in '38."

"No one saw him anymore after '38, but he was alive and busy in his laboratory near the train station, rumor had it. The Americans—or it might have been the Canadians—bombed the station in '44, and by chance a bomb fell on their laboratory, killing everyone inside. Junior was not there, and he continued his experiments for a short period of time after the war with money from the Russians. Bad science should not go to waste."

"Did the Allies target his lab?"

"Who knows?" Dr. Valo shrugged as he refilled our glasses with champagne. "Their laboratories were a big secret, but some of the doctors knew about them and what they were doing. They didn't have many friends in this town." He thought for a moment and said, "Maybe I'm wrong—it was the Germans who bombed their laboratory in the fall of '44. They knew about the Hellinherrs' laboratory and what they were doing there. What do you know? They destroyed the evidence."

"You said he had another lab?"

"Yes. It is speculated that it might be under the *Politechnica*, but no one knows for sure."

He and Tudor saw my raised eyebrows. "That's our Polytechnic University, near the Opera House," said Tudor.

"I see. Do you know what kind of experiments they performed?" I asked.

"Officially, if it was ever mentioned, it had to do with healing wounds faster. Unofficially, they were experimenting with life longevity. I also heard, but I don't believe it, that they were trying to discover a serum for immortality." Dr. Valo shook his head in disbelief.

"I don't see anything wrong with immortality," said Tudor.

"Immortality is fine, if it can be achieved. It was the people they used to perform their experiments on—I heard no one came out alive from their laboratories," Dr. Valo said. "Are you searching for their labs, Cat?"

I shook my head. "I was just curious about them, from what I had heard from my great-grandfather. But I thought they practiced in the open, not in secret labs."

"No. No one I know ever stepped in their laboratories. I hope my memories of them were helpful." Valo took a sip of his champagne.

"Thank you, Dr. Valo. It was great information. Like I said, I was just curious."

"Funny thing," Dr. Valo continued. "I don't think that I ever saw a picture of them after junior immigrated to America. Very few people remember them or what they looked like."

"Well, shall we have dinner?" asked Voichita.

And everything went well for the rest of the evening, until Tudor took me back to my hotel. He stopped the car at the entrance, and I was about to thank him for a lovely time when, from the corner of my eye, I saw a dark figure near a building close by. I got out to verify what I had seen, but one moment he was there and the next he wasn't. It was the same silhouette I had glimpsed earlier that day in front of the Opera House. He had moved with the speed and the stealth of a vampire.

Chapter 4

"Something the matter?" Tudor asked, seeing me get out of the car so quickly.

I got back into the car. "I don't know. I thought I saw someone familiar. Maybe it was just my imagination." I shook my head. "Tudor, I had a great time with Dr. Valo and his wife, and especially with you. I like you. You're a very pleasant man. Thank you."

"You're more than welcome." He took my hand and kissed it. He knew the old ways, too, and I liked that even more. "Tomorrow you will leave?"

I nodded.

"You'll drive yourself or do you have someone to take you to Sighisoara?"

"I have a driver and a tour guide, the driver's wife. She works for one of the travel agencies here in town."

"What are their names?"

"Dorin and Stanca Ionescu, I believe."

"The same fellow who was waiting for you at the clinic today?"

"Yes, that's him. Why?"

"No reason. I didn't recognize him, and by their name it sounds as if they are from Bucharest."

"Is that a problem?" I asked.

He shook his head.

"Wait, how could you remember two people from your city of 300,000 inhabitants?"

"I travel a lot. I know all the travel agents, and her name is not familiar."

"What are you trying to say?" I was slightly worried.

"Not to worry. I'm sure it's nothing." He looked at me with his gorgeous green eyes, and I saw some concern there. "You will have an empty seat in your car tomorrow, right?"

"Yes, I think so."

"What if I joined you on your trip to Sighisoara?"

"What?" I looked at him, puzzled, and probably with a hint of excitement that I would get to see him some more, but . . . "You don't have to worry about me. You're a busy man."

"It is rather slow at the clinic. Besides, there are other doctors. And spending a little time with you in Transylvania would be nice. If you don't mind?"

"You're so sweet. OK, but I'm paying for everything. I'll see you tomorrow morning at eight o'clock." I gave him a quick peck on the cheek and exited before something else could happen. As I entered the hotel's foyer, I looked back over my shoulder and saw a big smile on Tudor's face.

In the hotel lobby, I spotted the man from the Opera House, the blond dandy, but now he was wearing a black tuxedo with a black bow tie. He sat on a sofa looking away from me, as if he were expecting someone. Maybe he was here for an amorous dinner?

Once in my room, I called my vampire friend. "Hey, Mundibuto. What's going on?"

"Cat, how're you doing? I've rented a car and I'll leave tomorrow for Sighisoara," he said in his deep voice.

"Good. I'll be leaving tomorrow, too. I've hired a driver and a tour guide. Their names are Dorin and Stanca Ionescu. Also, I made a new friend, Dr. Tudor Lupu. He will join me on the trip."

"A doctor, eh! Is he good-looking?"

"Nosy! Yes, he's cute. But I called you to tell you something else. I saw, twice today, a man who reminded me very much of Vlad."

"Well, you know all these Romanians look alike." He chuckled.

"Seriously. I think this man is a vampire."

"What do you expect? You're in Transylvania. There ought to be some vampires, even in the city you are in now."

"This has nothing to do with me spotting him. Just this evening, when I saw him again, it looked as if he were spying on me."

"Hmmm. In that case, he might be one of Eleonore von Schwarzenberg's vampires, keeping an eye on you."

"Eleonore von Schwarzenberg, the self-appointed queen of vampires?"

"Yes, that's her. I should have met you in Timisoara," he said as an afterthought. "Stay safe until I meet you in Sighisoara."

"I will. But you know what? Why don't you shadow me once we arrive in Sighisoara? And thanks, Mundibuto."

The next morning, Tudor was in the lobby with one small bag, ready to accompany me on the trip to Transylvania and wearing the same smile as last night. I wondered if he had ever stopped smiling—or washed his cheek.

"Good morning, Tudor," I said cheerfully, dragging my bag behind me.

"Good morning, Cat. How are you today?"

"Excited about the trip ahead."

"Good morning, Miss Cat," said Dorin, entering the foyer. An attractive, auburn-haired woman in her early forties was by his side. "This is my wife and your tour guide, Stanca." We shook hands.

"Call me Cat. And I decided to take another passenger along." I motioned to Tudor. "This is Dr. Tudor Lupu. You may know him. Tudor, these are Dorin and Stanca Ionescu." As I was making the introductions, I registered a fleeting discontent in Dorin's and Stanca's eyes. But they immediately cheered up and shook hands with Tudor.

Tudor introduced himself, mentioning the name of his clinic. I didn't see any hint of recognition from Stanca. Maybe she didn't know his clinic, even though it was centrally located. Dorin didn't remark one way or the other, although he had taken me there. Could Tudor have been right, that these two were new in town?

We accommodated ourselves in the SUV Dorin had brought for the trip, a Dacia Duster, and since I was footing the bill, I got to sit in the front passenger seat. The SUV was spacious, so Tudor and Stanca had plenty of room in the back seat.

Stanca offered me a folder with brochures and points of interest to see in Transylvania, just for an American tourist like myself.

"I need to see Sighisoara first," I said. "After that, we can visit all these other wonderful places."

"Certainly," agreed Dorin. "We will be there by evening."

And so our trip began. Since the three Romanians spoke English, besides God knows how many other languages, we spoke English, my only language. I was an American, after all.

Stanca pointed out and described what we were seeing on our trip, including the ancient history of this land named Dacia, which was conquered by the Roman Emperor Trajan in the year 106. The Romans pillaged enough gold from Dacia to build another forum in Rome, the Trajan's forum. For more than a century ancient Transylvania was under the rule of the Roman Empire, and it was long enough to change the local language into a Romance language, as Romanian language is today. I learned that "Transylvania" means *beyond the forest*. And there were lots of forests around us, especially on the hilly terrain and mountains. Later and up to the Middle Ages, many migrating tribes came from the east. The Huns, ancestors of the Hungarians, settled east of Transylvania and conquered it. The Ottomans wanted this land, too, and occupied portions of it for a time. In more modern times, Transylvania was part of the Austro-Hungarian Empire until the end of the First World War, after which it became part of Romania. There were many other ethnic groups in Transylvania besides Romanians, such as Hungarians, Germans, Jews, and Gypsies. I hoped there wouldn't be a quiz, after all that information.

The land was beautiful, green with pastures on the rolling hills where cows and sheep were grazing lazily. Rivers, now overflowing from the recent storms, meandered through the valleys, with many villages that time seemed to have almost forgotten. Rather frequently, I saw ruins on the tops of hills, old remains of fortresses, castles, or monasteries strategically positioned to defend against enemies of the past. The closer we got to the heart of Transylvania, the rockier and taller the Carpathian Mountains grew.

We stopped for a late lunch in Alba Iulia, an important fortress town in the old days, where the complete reunification of Romania took place in 1918, Stanca informed me.

"What do you think of Transylvania?" Tudor asked me over lunch.

"It is beautiful. I never thought it would be this way." I was really impressed.

"The best is yet to come," Tudor said.

"Certainly," said Dorin. "Next stop is Sighisoara." He looked up at the sky unhappily, which was full of menacing clouds. "I predict more rain."

"But it will pass," said Stanca. "Why do you have to stop in Sighisoara first?"

I knew I had made a mistake by insisting so adamantly that I had to get to Sighisoara right away. I had raised their curiosity, and now I had to give them a reason to satisfy that curiosity. "I'm going to meet someone there tomorrow." I didn't elaborate, and Stanca didn't press for more information.

Stanca and Dorin excused themselves to go to the restrooms. Tudor and I were alone at the table.

"Have you been here before?" I asked Tudor.

"Yes. There are many historical sites to see. Did you make the arrangements for this trip with them?" He motioned with his head in the direction Dorin and Stanca had taken.

"I called my travel agent in New York, and she made the arrangements. Why?"

"Stanca texted a lot while we were driving here."

I raised my eyebrows. "Maybe she's a busy agent, with many friends and acquaintances." I shrugged.

"Perhaps, but she did most of the texting and received very few replies."

"What's on your mind, Tudor?"

"I shouldn't be so suspicious."

"Come on, tell me what worries you."

"For one thing, they don't seem to be who they say they are." He furrowed his brow. "Casually, I asked her about her education. She's from Bucharest, and that's where she received her degree in history—at the University of Bucharest, she says. The problem is that she didn't know certain well-known professors there."

"You're saying she's not what she claims to be." I glanced in the direction they had taken. "She seems to know her history."

"Most of the stuff she told us was from a tour guide to Transylvania." He smirked. "I don't think she works in the travel business. And as far as

33

Dorin goes, he has more education than he claims to have."

"Should I be worried? Who do you think they are?"

"If they are who I think they are, that will raise the question of who you are."

"You didn't answer my question." I leaned my elbows on the table and cupped my chin, looking inquisitively at him.

"Secret agents." He looked at me without blinking. "And they are not married, at least not to each other."

It was interesting that he had deduced all that. He was right: Stanca and Dorin could very well be secret agents requested by one of the US intelligence agencies to keep an eye on me and my business here in Transylvania. US Homeland Security was not convinced that my great-grandfather, Vlad V Draculesti, was dead, and maybe they hoped to find him in Transylvania while tailing me. How much easier could it be to have two agents impersonate a driver and a tour guide? It was quite possible.

And the question in Tudor's mind was: Who was I to raise the interest of the Romanian Secret Service? Good question.

"In case you don't know, I'm the heiress of a very rich man. Dorin and Stanca and their employer may want to know what a filthy-rich girl like me is doing in Romania." I winked at him.

"I hope that's the reason. Because there has been a black sedan following us since we left Timisoara."

That I didn't know. To him, the black sedan might have been the secret agents' back-up, but it made me think of the dark figure I had seen twice in Timisoara. "Really?" I showed my surprise.

"Dorin knew about it—I saw him checking his rearview mirror. Then I saw that same dark sedan, a BMW, several times, too."

"In that case, I'm glad you volunteered to join me on this trip." I caressed his face gently. He was too cute and caring not to receive my affection. He held my hand and kissed my palm. That felt electrifying.

Dorin and Stanca returned to the table and saved me. All of us walked to our car, and as we were about to get in, Tudor nodded to me, pointing an inconspicuous finger at a nearby street. There was a black sedan parked there.

Chapter 5

I couldn't see the driver in the car, but he could have been hiding behind the dashboard. I had a feeling that the man I had spotted twice in Timisoara was the driver. It was uncanny how much he resembled Vlad.

We departed for Sighisoara. Under the pretense of powdering my nose, I used my compact mirror to see if the car was following us. Sure enough, the black sedan came out from that street and turned left to follow us. From the corner of my eye, I noticed Dorin checking the rearview mirror. In my compact mirror I saw Tudor nodding knowingly to me.

The rest of the drive was uneventful, only with occasional downpours and lightning, punctuated by the sight of quaint villages in the hills, old churches, ruins, stork nests on chimneys, and historical places that Stanca pointed out. The black sedan passed us at one point, never to be seen again. Its windows were tinted dark, and I couldn't see who the driver was. Maybe it was our imagination that we were being followed.

"We'll be in Sighisoara in a few minutes," Stanca announced.

It was late in the day, shortly after sunset, but the dark clouds above changed the dusk into complete night. As we came around a bend in the road, a bolt of lightning illuminated the medieval rooflines of a town on the hill ahead, including a sharply pointed tower. Briefly, a moment later, the clouds cleared, allowing some of the last evening light to break through, and then I saw a scene worthy of a Dracula movie. Up the hill, with low banks of fog emanating from the soggy ground, among the many tile roofs, the Sighisoara Clock Tower loomed over us.

The tower's silhouette emerged macabre against the gray-crimson sky. It was a square tower, with a steep roof projecting up into an onion-dome shape and a spire shooting into the sky, as if it were a stake ready to impale its victim. On each corner of its roof stood a mini tower with an equally painful-looking sharp spike. It was frightening, disturbing, and beautiful to look at it.

"Oh my God!" I couldn't help my surprise at the grandiose sight above us. "This is so Dracula." I squirmed, thinking how painful would be to fall on one of those spikes.

Dorin couldn't stop the car, as there was only a ditch on the side of the road, but he slowed down to allow me to gawk at the sight. I reached quickly for my phone, but by the time I found it and aimed it at the tower, the clouds had closed in again and the ground fog began engulfing the tower. I gulped, trying to cement in my mind the eerie sight I had just witnessed.

"Wait until you see it tomorrow, in daylight," said Stanca.

I kept on looking back to see more of it, but the darkness and the fog obscured it from my view. I have vampire friends, my great-great-great grandfather was a vampire, and I had witnessed some horrific killings carried out by my vampire friends, but those things did not spook me as much as the image of that tower, the dusky light, the threateningly cloudy sky, and the wispy fog surrounding it.

"It was awesome," I said more to myself than the others. Our car stopped, yanking me out of my stupefaction.

"Here we are," said Dorin. "Your Olde Transylvania Inn."

Your Olde Transylvania Inn was old, all right, and it must have been an inn for many centuries, judging by the aged brown wood framing the exterior and the peeling paint on once-white-washed walls. Its name was on a wooden plank sign, squeaking on its hooks as the wind moved it.

Stanca must have seen my concerned face at the sight of this quaint, but nevertheless dumpy, inn, because she said, "It is an old inn, but it has been remodeled inside, and it has all the modern amenities, including indoor plumbing."

I smiled. What did I expect? Sighisoara was a medieval town, at least the part we were in. "I'm sorry. I didn't mean to act all prissy. This fits perfectly with the ambiance I expected." The indoor plumbing part she had mentioned was reassuring.

The owner, a gray-haired man, came out and bowed to us. Stanca conversed with him, and two lads emerged from the office to help us with our baggage. I gave the owner my credit card, and Stanca filled out the forms for our lodging.

Tudor engaged the owner in an animated discussion, and I wondered what the fuss was all about. "Would you believe this?" Tudor said to me. "There are no vacancies anywhere in Sighisoara."

"I'm sorry," said Stanca. "But I presumed that you had already taken care of your hotel accommodations."

"No." He sighed. "I didn't think about it. I expected to find a room in one of the many hotels around here." He turned to the owner and discussed alternatives, while the owner nodded understandingly. "I'll be renting a car to go to Targu Mures, where I'll find some accommodations," Tudor concluded. I felt sorry he did not have a room nearby.

I followed the bellboy up the stairs to my second-story room on an outside corridor overlooking the open courtyard. The room was quaint and charmingly decorated, just like a room at an inn should be, especially on this stormy evening. My room had two twin beds.

I stepped outside my room and saw that Dorin and Stanca had accommodations on the first floor, at the base of the stairs, as if to keep an eye on me.

I returned to the office where Tudor was waiting for a taxi. He smiled bravely at me. "Well, I guess I'll see you tomorrow morning," he said.

"Tudor, listen. I have two beds in my room," I said hesitantly. Tudor raised his eyebrows. "If you promise to behave like a gentleman, I'll let you use one of them."

Tudor rubbed the back of his neck and looked outside, where the rain had begun falling again. "Due to the circumstances, I'll accept. And I promise that my mother will be proud of me." We both smiled at each other.

He said the right thing. If he had said that his father would be proud of him, the deal would be off. "Get your bag and come upstairs." I left him in the office to cancel his arrangements, and I waited for him outside my room.

As he started up the stairs, Dorin came out of his room and they discussed something in Romanian. Dorin didn't seem pleased by the new course of events, but since I was footing the bill and he was not my father, he had to accept it. Tudor came up to my room, rolling his eyes about Dorin's comments. "Big Brother is watching," he whispered as he stepped inside the room.

From the upper level, I called down to Dorin, "Where are we going to have dinner?"

He exchanged a few words with Stanca through the open door of his room. "The Inn's restaurant. Is ten minutes sufficient for you to get ready for dinner?"

"OK." I remained outside and telephoned Mundibuto. "Hey, we've arrived in Sighisoara. I'm staying at Your Olde Transylvania Inn."

"Hey, Cat. I'm in Brasov now, not too far from where you are."

"It seems there are no vacancies here in town."

"I just reserved a room near the tower at Dracula's Inn. My kind of place."

I chuckled. "I bet. Freshly shifted dirt on every casket."

"I'm not that kind of vampire. Do you need to meet with me tonight?"

"No. I'm good. Well, we'll be having dinner soon."

"Yeah, I'll be having a bite to eat, too. Some roadside place. I haven't made up my mind who to have—Romanian, Hungarian, or German? Or maybe Gypsy? I think I'll try that." He burst out in a deep laugh.

Morbid, but true. He was a vampire, and human blood was a necessity for vampires, an essential life elixir that kept them young. He had to get it from some unsuspecting woman or man, and he could do it without she or he even knowing that a vampire had sucked their blood. The fact was that real vampires never killed any of their victims, and the victims would never become vampires. Also, blood was not what nourished them; alcohol was his and all vampires' nourishment.

And it was time for my nourishment as well. We went to the Inn's restaurant, which judging by its fireplace, was as old as the Inn. I expected to see at any minute Gandalf and his dwarfs walk in. But there were only tourists in the low-ceilinged tavern.

Since I was in Transylvania, I had to taste some of the local cuisine, so I ordered *sarmale*—stuffed cabbage with pork, and *mamaliga*, a corn meal dish. I'd never had it before, but it was good. I even had a taste of *tsuica*, a plum brandy that I didn't particularly like. The Romanian red wine was quite good. We finished our dinner with a slice of *cozonac*, a roll filled with ground walnuts and raisins, and sour-cherry liqueur, *vishinata*, which was not sour at all.

The dinner and the conversation was pleasant, until Stanca asked me, "Who are you going to meet here in Sighisoara?"

Yes, they were definitely trying to find my great-grandfather Vlad V. "I don't know, but when I see her I'll recognize her."

"Her? Wasn't it a man?" Stanca asked, disbelieving.

"A man?" I acted confused. "No, I'm supposed to find a fortune teller," I lied.

Chapter 6

Returning from dinner, I suspected something was different about the room, and I walked around, wishing I had a listening-device detector. In our absence, someone had been in there.

"Which bed do you want?" Tudor asked, watching me with interest.

"The one near the bathroom." I placed a finger over my lips to tell Tudor not to talk. I kept searching for any visible microphones. I found none. I went into the bathroom to check it out. The shower stall had a tub and was enclosed by a curtain. It was a possibility, if I needed to have a private conversation.

I returned to the bedroom and, looking at Tudor, I pointed to my phone. It was time to exchange some words with him, in silence. I texted: <This room may b bugged.>

Tudor looked surprised when he saw my message. While looking around the room, he cupped his hand behind his ear, verifying that I was talking about listening devices.

I nodded and said, "Have you visited Sighisoara before?"

"Several times, when I was younger." His text reply: <What's going on? How do u know?>

I replied: <I have a feeling. Dorin and Stanca r listening to us. Talk about frivolous stuff.>

"Yeah. Every time I visit this place, it is like going back in time." He leaned back on his pillow and texted: <Who are u? Why the spy stuff?>

Now came the difficult part: How do I explain to him that all I wanted to do was to spread Vlad's ashes from the tower tomorrow at midnight? But then, how do I— spied on by the Romanian Secret Service and pursued by someone in a black sedan— allay his suspicions? He was probably thinking that this had to do with something far bigger than me just being a rich girl.

"Do you mind if I turn the radio on?" He shook his head, and I turned it on. A little background music would cover our long gaps in discussion.

I texted him: <No spy stuff. I am here to spread my g-father's ashes from the tower.>

He replied: <Why?>

<His wishes. He was from here.>

<Then why r u being watched?>

I inhaled and texted back: <US Homeland Security wants my g-father. Nothing illegal. They believe that my g-father is still alive. I could lead them to him.>

<Is he dead?>

From the bottom of my bag I pulled out the jar with Vlad's ashes and showed it to him.

Tudor texted: <Are those his ashes?>

"Yes," I said. "I can barely wait to see Sighisoara tomorrow in daylight."

"In that case, I'll settle in. We will have a busy day tomorrow." Tudor pulled off the bed covers.

We tucked ourselves into our respective beds, like brother and sister. I wore my cotton pajamas with the long pants. He was in a T-shirt and boxer shorts. He had a cute butt. I wondered if he had

46

checked out my butt. Did he think that it was too big? Or that my breasts weren't big enough? I chased those girlish thoughts out of my mind. But why? I was 23 years old, for crying out loud. And he was a hunk.

"Do you snore?" I asked.

"I'm not sure, but all the windows in my bedroom are intact when I wake up every morning." He chuckled.

"Then my eardrums are safe. Good night, then."

"Good night, Cat. I'll do some light reading, if you don't mind." He began tapping on his tablet.

"Not at all." I turned away from him and tried to go to sleep. A few minutes later, though, he called my name. I looked over at him. He was holding his tablet up for me to see. It displayed my picture. He had checked my background over the Internet.

"So you are the great-granddaughter of Vlad V Draculesti, the billionaire?" he asked.

"Yes."

"You must be very rich."

"Yes."

"What are you doing here, by yourself?"

"What do you mean? Whom should I be with?"

"Bodyguards. What if you are kidnapped?"

"But I'm not by myself. You are with me. And Dorin and Stanca are with us as well."

"Huh. That's right. We are with you."

"Besides, who in Transylvania would know who I am?"

"You may be surprised. Have you ever heard of Gypsies?"

"Yeah, but they're pickpockets, not kidnappers."

"I'm talking about Gypsy organized-crime groups, and not only from Romania, but from Bulgaria, Ukraine, and even Russia."

I smiled at him. He looked cute, all concerned about my safety. "Let them try." I turned away. It may have come across as bravado on my part, but Tudor and, for that matter, Dorin and Stanca did not know what formidable bodyguards I had at my command. They are the Strigoi, another inheritance from Vlad. In fact, the name is Romanian and it means "ghosts." And they are ghostly apparitions that, in case of danger, manifest themselves and take actions on my behalf to protect me. When my life was in danger from the vampire slayers' cult back in New York, the Strigoi killed them all. After that, I felt well-protected.

My phone vibrated. Mundibuto texted: <R u asleep. I am in town.>

I texted back: <Awake. It seems the Rom Scrt Srvice is monitoring me. My driver and guide r agents. Shadow me for now.>

Mundibuto texted: <OK.>

<I am with my Dr friend.>

<Where is he now?>

<In the next bed.>

<In the same room with u?>

<Yes. He's OK.>

I imagined what Mundibuto must have been thinking about my safety. Or maybe not my safety, but about me, being such a playgirl. Maybe Mundibuto was right to be concerned about my safety. Was Tudor who he said he was? I felt no threat from him, but . . . Trust but verify. Tudor had checked me out over the Internet; I had to do the same with him.

He was who he said he was: a doctor working for the emergency clinic in Timisoara. Even his picture matched. That part was good; now I could go to sleep.

My phone vibrated again. Tudor texted me: <Vlad V Draculesti. Who is this guy?>

I replied: <My great-grandfather.>

<Draculesti is the family name of Vlad the Impaler. Dracula.>

<Yes, I know.>

<He was Dracula, the vampire?>

<Yes, Dracula. And I have his ashes in the jar.>

It took a few seconds to sink in, but then Tudor burst out laughing. "Good night, Cat."

Sometimes the truth is more unbelievable than a lie.

Chapter 7

I woke up the next morning to find Tudor already up and reading the news on his tablet. I hadn't heard him taking his shower, but he was fresh and dressed for the coming day.

"Good morning," I said, feeling a bit embarrassed for sleeping late. My hair was probably a mess, which didn't help the situation.

"Good morning, Cat. How did you sleep?"

"Soundly. I didn't hear you snoring."

"But I heard you." He snickered.

"No way! I don't snore."

"No, you don't. But you talk in your sleep."

"What did I say?"

"You mentioned a name. I think you said François. Who's he?" Tudor sounded a bit jealous.

"A good friend." I smiled, wondering what dreams I had had about my gorgeous vampire friend. "Did I say anything else?"

"No, that was all."

I ran to the bathroom to get ready for the day.

While in the bathroom, I texted Tudor: <Midnight, tower, spread Vlad's ashes. Any ideas how to do that?>

Tudor texted back: <Not open to visitors at night. I'll think of something.>

If Tudor couldn't help me, I was sure Mundibuto would be able to, somehow. I texted Mundibuto: <Hey. R u up?>

He replied: <Sure am. I've been watching your room. U not kidding u r with a man.>

I texted back: <U got me. And he's a Dr.>

<Good for u. Today plan?>

<Recon mission. Spread Vlad's ashes from tower, midnight. Tower closed at night.>

He replied: <I'll take u there.>

I imagined Mundibuto, with me on his back, climbing the tower's stonewalls at night. I shouldn't worry, though. It would be just 100 feet or so to the observation deck. Plus, he's a vampire. He can't fall—maybe. I think he's going to be my plan B.

I texted: <I asked Tudor 4 help 2. Maybe he knows people.>

He replied: <Let me know if u need help.>

Outside on the street, the air was fresh, cleansed by the rain. The storm had passed, although big white clouds filled the sky, allowing the sun to shine down most of time. We met up with Dorin and Stanca, and we all went to an outdoor café for breakfast. While we were eating, Tudor and I became convinced that Dorin and Stanca had listened in on our conversations of the night before. But they didn't discover any secrets, and little did they know what Tudor and I were planning at midnight. From our conversation, I got the feeling that Dorin was baffled that Tudor hadn't made a move on me. It just showed where his mind was— and he called himself a married man, and to Stanca!

We admired the old Sighisoara architecture from our table. In the daylight, the Clock Tower did not look so menacing. It was a beautiful structure, built from stone for the purpose of watching over the fields for the Turkish invaders of long ago. The roof was colorful but aged, with geometric designs made of glazed clay tiles. The onion-dome shapes at the top, the big center one and the other four smaller ones at each corner of the roof, were clad in copper, weathered to a dull green. The black spires looked as sharp and ominous as they had last night. Just below the roof's eaves, the observation deck was open on all sides for 360-degree views over the surrounding area. A large clock dial was located below the deck. The tower narrowed slightly below the clock, giving the impression of a square tulip head.

Walls, ramparts, and old houses with orange tile roofs surrounded the tower. Originally, Sighisoara had been a citadel, a fort on the hill to protect the city and its inhabitants from invaders. Now, it was just a quaint medieval town, occupying the hill down to the road below and beyond. The top of the hill was crowned with a Gothic church, where the Transylvanian Saxon-Germans worshipped.

After breakfast, we started up the street toward the citadel. Across a small plaza at an outdoor café, Mundibuto, with dark sunglasses and a brimless African cap, was sipping an alcoholic drink. On the table, a half-full bottle of a clear liquid awaited its demise.

Tudor stared at him, and I arched my eyebrows, questioning his puzzlement. "You know what that black guy is drinking?" he whispered discreetly in my ear.

I shook my head.

"He's drinking *palinca*. That's a plum brandy. One hundred proof. Not a good way to start your day." He shook his head in dismay over that fellow's health.

Not a good way, for sure, unless you were a vampire and having breakfast. Mundibuto's muscular body dwarfed the table in front of him. I felt better seeing him and knowing that he would be watching out for me, although he was very conspicuous—he was the only African around, and the only one drinking *palinca* at that hour.

The narrow, cobblestoned medieval street, surrounded by houses built centuries ago, curved upward toward the arched open gate of the Clock Tower. We walked right through the tower, which straddled the street. This must have been one of the citadel's entrances, which at night would have been closed by heavy wooden gates. Now the gates were long gone. Past the tower, enclosed behind the walls of the fortress, an old medieval town opened up. Most of the houses were two or even three stories high, with steep and ornate orange clay tile roofs.

"Sighisoara, although it has been invaded and burned down in the past and then reconstructed, has remained the same since medieval times," Stanca said.

"People still live here, in the old town?" I asked.

"Yes, they do," she answered. "That is the City Hall." She pointed to the massive, three-storied building on our right, with its steep roof and many towers. "That was a noble's castle, once upon a time."

"Dracula's?" I asked innocently.

"No. But this building claims to have housed Vlad the Impaler in his travels from Transylvania to Walachia." She pointed to the dark-yellow building ahead of us on the left, which proudly displayed its historical notoriety on a marble plaque on its wall, right under an ornate sign with a golden dragon on it that advertised a restaurant and brewery.

The Clock Tower's bell rang ten times. It was 10 o'clock. The figurines next to the clock's dial came out of their porticoes and rotated around. A town crier, dressed in the medieval attire of tights, long-tipped shoes, red and black striped bloomers, a red tunic, and a fluffy hat with a pheasant feather in it, welcomed tourists in several languages.

"Can we go up into the tower?"

"By all means," Stanca replied.

While purchasing our tickets, I noticed the hours the tower was open: 9:00 to 19:00. As I had thought: no tourists were allowed inside at midnight. Dorin stayed behind, uninterested in the climb to the top, and checked his messages. The rest of us headed for the stairway, passing through four-foot thick walls. The interior of the tower was hollow, a square shaft containing the heavy wooden stairs that led to the top. After several minutes and many turns, we arrived at the summit. What a view!

Now I could see why Vlad had wanted his ashes spread from the tower. Behind us was the old town and in front was the Plain of Albesti, where many battles had taken place, according to Stanca.

After I had satisfied my touristic curiosity and taken enough pictures with my phone, I began inspecting the deck from where I was supposed to throw the ashes. There was only one way here, up these stairs and through the heavy door at the bottom, which was locked at night. The deck was encircled by a heavy railing and was open all around under the roof. Thick wooden columns supported the pyramidal tile roof and spire above. I looked down over the railing, but because the deck section of the tower protruded outward, I couldn't see the wall below. Looking down to the street from this height gave me vertigo.

There was no way for anyone to climb up the wall of the tower.

After the tower visit, we walked through the old streets of the town and mingled with the tourists searching for Dracula souvenirs in the local shops. Besides the mandatory Dracula pictures and vampire paraphernalia, the shops offered local artisanal woodcarvings, colorful pottery, leather belts, and sheepskin vests and hats. Sighisoara was a place that time had forgotten. Next to the tower on the right side was a Catholic church, on another street was a Romanian Orthodox church, and up on the hill was the impressive Gothic church.

We took a steep, covered pathway to the top of the hill to see the Gothic church. The shade from the pergola and the vines growing on it provided some coolness as we walked up. The church was worth the climb. The stone floor inside was worn down from the many centuries of worshippers who had walked there. Many religious paintings of

Christ, Virgin Mary and Child, and the Appostoles adorned the walls. I prayed and lit three candles: two for my parents and one for Vlad.

"There's a cemetery next to the church. Would you like to see it?" Stanca asked when we were again outside.

"Anything interesting there?" I asked. Just then, I noticed a dark figure among the marble angel statues, crosses, and obelisks.

"Just an old cemetery, with mausoleums and many statues," said Stanca.

Ordinarily, I probably would not have wanted to visit the old cemetery, but I was curious about the man I was seeing again. I walked quickly to the place among the marble-clad graves where I saw the dark figure. It was easy to spot him in his black attire, moving among the white, weather-beaten marble shapes. But as quickly as he had appeared, he disappeared again in the vicinity of a Greco-Roman-style mausoleum with black marble columns.

Chapter 8

Stanca and Dorin were looking at me strangely, watching me dart among the graves and stopping in front of the mausoleum, turning around in place and retracing my steps as if I were lost.

"What happened?" asked Tudor, coming after me.

I didn't answer him, and continued walking around the mausoleum, hoping to spot that man. There was no one around other than us. I walked to the heavy front doors and I pulled and pushed on the brass rings that served as handles, but to no avail. The door was locked with heavy chains, so it seemed unlikely that he had gone inside.

"Zis is private mausoleum, no open to public," said a voice behind me, speaking English well-enough that I could understand him. He seemed to be the groundskeeper. The man was in his thirties, rough and unshaven. Despite the summer heat, he had on a black fur cap, bent to one side. He wore a dirty white shirt, a worn leather vest, and dark workpants. His brown boots were muddy from the wet soil of the cemetery paths.

"I'm sorry," I said. "Have you seen a man dressed in black walking around here?"

The man smiled crookedly and scratched the side of his unshaven face. "No. Maybe you see *strigoi*?"

Strigoi—ghosts. No, I knew what strigoi looked like, and the man I had seen was not a ghost. "Thank you. Sorry to bother you." I smiled at him and returned to my companions, who were gawking at me. They were probably thinking, *crazy American girl*.

The man didn't take his eyes off me. I deliberately walked behind Dorin and Stanca, and the man kept staring at me, unblinking, unflinching. This man was a vampire. His worn-out attire and neglected grooming masked his true vampire identity. There was one sure way to verify my suspicion.

I turned around and approached him again, extending my hand. "Hello, my name is Cat. What is your name?" He took my hand reluctantly, but I made sure I had his palm fully in my grasp—a cold, reptilian hand. The hand of a vampire. It sent a chill up my spine to realize that I was meeting a Transylvanian vampire.

"My name is Nicolae." He stopped smiling. His eyes were cold and dark.

This crude man-vampire made me uneasy. I pulled my hand quickly out of his grip, afraid that he might crush it. "Nice to meet you, Nicolae. Are you from around here?"

"I is from all over." He gestured with his arm at the cemetery.

I tried to smile. "OK, 'bye." I made a hasty retreat, but when I turned and looked back, Nicolae was gone.

My phone rang. It was Mundibuto. "Hey," I said.

"I saw them. You don't need to talk. The rough-looking vampire is Nicolae. He is one of the three henchmen who helped the Turks decapitate Vlad the Impaler. The other vampire in black clothes and a cape looked very much like Vlad when he was young. I don't know who he is."

"What should I do?" I asked.

"Act naturally. Tonight, we'll spread Vlad's ashes, and then we must leave. Nicolae hated your great-grandfather Vlad."

Suddenly, I remembered: My great-grandfather had told me the story about the three traitors— Nicolae, Ilie, and Lazlo–who had helped the Turkish assassins decapitate Vlad the Impaler. The three Judases then were infected by Vlad the Impaler's blue blood and became vampires. My great-great-great-grandfather Vlad V killed Lazlo, the leader, and the other two hid themselves for all those centuries from Vlad V. And now here was Nicolae, and chances were good that he knew I was Vlad V Draculesti's progeny. I needed Mundibuto's help now more than ever. I wished François and Angelique, my other two vampire friends, were here as well. "OK." I disconnected our call, wondering if this was a coincidence or if they were waiting for me.

"Everything OK?" Tudor asked, as he saw me deep in thought.

"Yes, everything is fine." I smiled only with my lips, trying to hide my concern over the vampires' presence. The bell in the Gothic church rang 12 times. "Shall we have lunch?"

We walked down to the old town center and, in good tradition, we had lunch at Casa Vlad Dracula. Blood sausages were on the menu. There was not much conversation, as my thoughts were elsewhere. Stanca offered tidbits of information about Dracula, and I listened absentmindedly.

As soon as the lunch ended, Tudor stood up and said, "If you'd excuse me, I'd like to visit with an old colleague of mine here in Sighisoara." He winked at me.

"Sure," I said, wondering what he had in mind.

"He must have lost interest," said Dorin, watching Tudor depart.

"How are you and Tudor getting along?" Stanca asked.

That was rather nosy of her, but I had to maintain appearances. "He's a great guy. Very nice, as a matter of fact."

Dorin and Stanca exchanged knowing glances.

"Have you spotted the mysterious fortune-teller woman?" she asked.

"Someone played a practical joke on me. The call I received at the cemetery informed me that it was all a hoax."

"So that's why the long face," smirked Dorin.

"Yeah, I guess." I hoped they bought my lame lie.

"But look on the bright side—you're in Sighisoara," said Stanca, attempting to cheer me up.

These two were reading me. It was time to change tactics. "By the way, are you sure that there aren't vampires here in Transylvania?" I asked naively.

Chapter 9

Dorin almost choked on his coffee. Stanca laughed. "Those are just legends." She flipped her hand dismissively. "We don't have vampires, otherwise we would know about them."

As agents of the secret service or undercover police, they would have known if vampires were real, and to their knowledge they were not. Vampires didn't exist.

Later that evening, we had dinner in town, and after dinner Tudor announced, "I found a vacancy at the hotel in the old town. I won't have to impose on you any longer, Cat."

"Oh," I whimpered. I thought we had a good arrangement. I felt more secure with him in my room, but maybe he had difficulties keeping his promise to make his mother proud.

"That's great," said Stanca, as if she were pleased to see him out of the way.

Dorin raised an eyebrow in surprise. It seemed obvious that he thought Tudor was an idiot not to stay with me in my room again. But then he met Stanca's gaze, cleared his throat, and said, "Certainly."

"Well then, since I have the key, you'd better follow me to get your stuff," I said in an even tone.

We walked together back to our inn, and Tudor left after picking up his bag. I sat up in my bed, thinking about how I was going to get to the tower at midnight. Tudor couldn't help me, and I imagined Mundibuto scaling the wall with me on his back. He could break down the tower's door. No, that would be too noisy. I thought about Tudor again. I liked him. Why did he have to get his own room?

My phone vibrated. I had a text message from Tudor: <Hi, Cat. Sorry to leave u alone, but 1 escaping from the inn 2nite is easier than 2.>

I texted back: <Don't be silly. OK.>

He replied: <Good news. I have a key to the tower door.>

I sat up, all excited. Tudor had a key! I texted him: <How?>

<Connections. Meet u at 11:30 bottom of Tower Street. Can u get out without being followed?>

<Meet you there. Thanks.> I wanted to tell him that I'd give him a big kiss, but it would be better to do it in person rather than through a text message. I'd meet him at the bottom, walk to the tower, unlock the gate, and climb the stairs to the top, the civilized way. Good deal! I leaned back and placed my hands under my head, daydreaming for a while.

I texted Mundibuto: <Tudor has key to tower. I meet him at 11:30 bottom of Tower Street.>

He replied: <I have a key 2.>

So much for imagining that Mundibuto would have scaled the wall with me on his back! I laughed, thinking of my dramatic assumption.

I texted: <Good, thanks. Wait for us at tower base.>

He replied: <R u going up in tower with him?>

That was a good question. Yes, I would go with him. How else could I give him that kiss? And in a tower, at midnight, hopefully with full moon shining on us . . .

I texted back: <Yes.>

Mundibuto replied: <I keep an i on u. And him. And the other 2 vampires.>

He had a point about the other two vampires. Suddenly I didn't feel so romantic anymore. But Mundibuto would be at the base of the tower, and any vampires coming after us would have to get past him. I felt better.

And then Dorin and Stanca came to mind. How would I get out of my room without them knowing? I went to the bathroom window to check the back of the inn. The window was big enough to squeeze through. But it was two stories up, and the cold, hard cobblestoned street below was not welcoming.

I returned to my room and considered my alternatives. Bathroom window—no. Front door—no: Dorin and Stanca would know of my escape and would watch me from the bottom of the stairs, wondering where I was going at that time of night. I wouldn't be able to get rid of them. How about the front window? Yes, the window opened onto the outside corridor, and I could stealthily climb out through it, tip-toe to the stairs, and slip down quietly to the inner courtyard and then out into the street. Window—yes!

By 11:15, I was dressed in black for my midnight escapade, my backpack bag containing Vlad's ashes strapped securely on my back. I opened the window as quietly as possible and looked outside. All was silent, except for a cat in heat, which started crying like a baby. Under the cover of the amorous cat's teeth-jarring serenade, I climbed out through the window and squatted down in the corridor. Everything was quiet and calm. The cat took an intermission.

Stepping close to the wall, I moved slowly to the stairs, and I got there without a sound. At the stairs I had to make another decision: Should I run down like a bat out of hell and dash into the street, or descend carefully so as not to make the stairs creak? Then an idea hit me—why not slide down the bannister and run to my rendezvous spot? And so I took a deep breath, placed my derriere on the railing, and pushed off.

Halfway down the bannister, the darn thing cracked and then broke, dumping me over the rail. I quickly realized that I was going to end up head down and bottom up in the petunia flowerbed below the stairs. Thinking fast—at least in this dire situation—I pulled my knees up to my chest and flipped, managing to rotate and land feet-first in the petunias. My landing was quiet, but the stairs were completely uncooperative; the railing continued breaking, falling over and making a racket like dominos.

I made a run for the street and once out of the inn, I squatted down near the outside wall and looked back. Dorin and Stanca were outside their room, wondering what was going on. I saw Stanca running up the stairs to my room and knocking at my door. Dorin came out into the street. In the dim light, I saw a gun in his hand. I hid behind a small bush. He searched the street with a flashlight and was about to shine it into where I was hiding, when Stanca called after him and he ran up the stairs.

My absence had been discovered. I sprinted to the nearest corner, turned, and raced away. I tried to put as much distance between me and the inn as possible. The commotion of the breaking railing woke up the neighborhood dogs, and their barking muffled the sound of my footsteps.

I took a longer route to my appointed destination, and I arrived there at 11:35. I was late, but Tudor was not there.

Chapter 10

Tudor had stood me up. Did he leave once he realized I was late? Maybe he walked back to the inn? I called him on my phone: "Tudor, where are you?"

"I'm in my room," he answered in a sulking voice.

"What are you doing in your room? You were supposed to meet me here at the bottom of Tower Street."

"Yes, yes, but I lost the key. I'm looking for it, but I'll meet you at the tower's door as soon as I find it."

I disconnected and ran up the street, panting as I arrived at the door. It was 11:45 pm. A light fog hovered at street level. I looked around for Tudor in the dim light and the mist. Nothing. Then I remembered that Mundibuto had a key as well. But where was he?

From the Dracula's Inn a couple of blocks away, a figure approached me. It was Tudor.

"Hurry up!" I urged him in a hushed voice. "Midnight's almost here."

"Cat, I'm sorry. I couldn't find the key." He sounded disappointed about letting me down.

My shoulders slumped. I checked my watch: It was 10 minutes to midnight. A light wind blew the fog away, but clouds obscured the full moon and, at that moment, it was completely dark. And it was good that it was dark. Tudor would not have liked to see the murderous expression on my face.

"Maybe you should try my key." A deep voice spoke from around the tower's corner. It was Mundibuto.

Tudor jumped almost as high as the tower at the sound of Mundibuto's voice, and he took a defensive stance when the large man approached us.

"Thank God, Mundibuto," I breathed in relief. "At least you didn't lose your key." I threw Tudor a displeased look, which again was lost in the dark.

"Heh, heh," snickered Mundibuto. "He didn't lose his key. I stole it from him."

"What?" I couldn't believe my ears. Mundibuto had stolen the key from Tudor, and Tudor was feeling like crap because he thought he had lost it, and here I was, ready to impale Tudor for losing the key. "Give me the darn thing! Time is short." I grabbed the key from Mundibuto and ran to the door.

"Who's he?" Tudor asked in a shaky voice.

"I'm sorry, Tudor. He's a friend. His name is Mundibuto. He's a pickpocket." I was pissed off, and my shaking hands couldn't find the keyhole.

"Allow me," said Mundibuto. He inserted the key and opened the door. "You want me to come with you?"

"I'll go with her," said Tudor, now recovered from his shock.

"Yes, Tudor, come with me." I turned my flashlight on and ran up the stairs.

"I'll be down here." I heard the hurt in Mundibuto's voice and the wooden door slamming shut behind us.

If there was a world record for getting to the observation deck at the top of this tower, I broke it for sure. It was 11:57 pm, just three minutes left to fulfill Vlad's wishes. I got there in the nick of time, lowered my backpack to the wood-planked floor, and removed the jar with Vlad's ashes. The ashes in the jar were luminescent, glowing a soft neon-blue. They were mesmerizing in the darkness.

Tudor finally managed to arrive at the deck, breathing heavily. He bent over, propping himself with his hands on his knees. Then he straightened up and stared at the glowing jar. Between deep breaths, he asked, "What . . . is . . . that?"

"My great-grandfather's ashes."

"Why . . . are . . . they . . . glowing?"

"I don't know. I never saw them glowing before. Or maybe I never looked at them in the dark before." I checked my watch. It was 11:59. The sky was covered with clouds. Was it supposed to be a clear full moon when I scattered his ashes, or was it good enough even if clouds obscured the moon?

The tower's bell above us rang once.

It startled me. The clock was sounding midnight, but suddenly there was light. The full moon, blindingly bright, came out of the clouds. The medieval roofs down below shined with silvery reflected light. Even here on the covered observation deck, the moonlight provided ample visibility.

The tower's bell sounded again.

It was time to fulfill Vlad's wishes. But I couldn't unscrew the lid off the jar. I gave it to Tudor, who had no problem opening it. Walking around the square deck, I scattered Vlad V Draculesti's ashes over the railing and over Sighisoara, while giving a short prayer to Vlad. I finished just as the twelfth sound of the hammer hit the bell above us.

It was done. Vlad's wishes had been fulfilled. The moon went dark, back into the clouds.

Tudor had recovered from his climbing effort and was breathing normally, which was good, considering what I was about to do. I went up to him and put my arms around his neck. "Thank you for your help, Tudor." I kissed him tenderly on his lips. My heart fluttered from being so close to him, touching his lips.

He was surprised but pleased, and quickly encircled his arms around my waist. He was a good kisser; his lips were soft and tasted sweet.

"And I'm sorry I was upset about you losing the key. It was not your fault." I kissed him again, and he kissed me back, for twice as long. He was a very good kisser. And I felt aroused and romantic and wild to be at the top of the Clock Tower in Transylvania, in Dracula's country. So we kept kissing.

Suddenly he took his lips away, and looked around us worriedly. Something unusual was happening. Around the deck a luminous blue cloud encircled the tower. I thought it was the moonlight, but the moon was hidden in the clouds. Vlad's ashes had become a phosphorescent haze. It surrounded the tower like an aura. We looked at it for a minute or so, fascinated but uneasy at what we were seeing.

"What did you scatter over the railing, Cat?" Tudor asked nervously.

"Ashes. My great-grandfather's ashes."

"Are those ashes radioactive?"

"Radioactive? Wouldn't that be green in color?"

"Not really."

I shook my head. "No, that's impossible. That's not radioactive. I was there when we incinerated him. And afterward we collected his ashes."

"Incinerated him? Don't you mean cremated?"

"Yes, yes. I meant cremated."

Tudor looked at me suspiciously. "You incinerated him because he was a biohazard?"

Tudor was making me uncomfortable. He had deduced from my words that we—Mundibuto, François, Angelique, and I—had indeed incinerated Vlad to destroy any trace of his vampire blue blood to prevent human infection. Yes, Vlad was a biohazard.

We heard a creaking sound nearby, and we froze.

"That was very, very interesting." A voice spoke from the head of the stairway. As the moon came out of the clouds again, it revealed a dark figure standing there. He was a tall, pale man with black slicked-back hair, deep black eyes, a straight narrow nose, and thin purple lips.

Incredibly, the dark figure was young Vlad.

Chapter 11

"Oh my God!" I covered my mouth with my hands. It couldn't be. My great-grandfather Vlad had died. I had witnessed that. I had seen his corpse incinerated. This man was a vampire resembling a younger Vlad. Had I been played for a fool and in reality Vlad had never died, only faking his age as an old man? Was all this to evade US Homeland Security and the NSA? But why involve me? Why was I caught in this game?

"Who are you?" I asked in a trembling voice.

"Vlad the Impaler." He smiled and showed his white teeth, his large canines retracted.

At least he didn't claim to be Vlad V, my great-grandfather. I felt better knowing that my great-grandfather was the vampire I thought he was and that I wasn't being used in some nefarious plot. I said, "Vlad the Impaler died long ago."

"I am the undead. I am a vampire. I am Dracula." He lifted his arms, displaying the red satin inside his black cape.

"Yes, you are a vampire. But you are not Dracula, and you are not the undead. You are quite alive. Who are you really?"

"I told you." He took a step closer to me. "Dracula," he hissed.

"You are an impostor. You are a fake Dracula. Fake-ula," I nicknamed him, placing my knuckles on my hips.

"Cat, what are you talking about?" Tudor asked in alarm, putting himself in front of me to shield me.

Tudor thought that this man was a demented guy in a costume instead of a real vampire.

"What do you want?" I asked Fakeula, pushing Tudor gently aside.

Instead of responding, he looked over the railing at the luminous haze created by the ashes. Part of it started drifting slowly toward the church and cemetery on top of the hill. The trailing part of the haze passed over the deck, engulfing us. Fakeula shrunk at its presence. With the agility of a cat, he jumped onto the roof's upper beams to avoid the luminous fog. A moment later, as the haze cleared, he dropped smoothly back down onto the deck. "What was in that jar?" he demanded.

"None of your business," I replied, convinced that I was well-protected by my Strigoi and Mundibuto down below in the street.

Fakeula moved toward us in two steps, grabbed Tudor by the throat with one hand, and lifted him up. "What was in the jar?" He focused on me with narrowed eyes.

"Mundibuto!" I screamed for his help, but Mundibuto did not respond nor jump to my rescue. It was time to call my Strigoi. I ran straight at Fakeula and grabbed him by his cold throat, knowing full well that I was no match for him. But I wanted him to hurt me so I could summon my Strigoi. He backslapped me on my right cheek, and I flew across the deck. I saw stars; my cheek hurt badly from the same wound that Tudor had stitched. I raised my arms, hands facing out, and shouted, "Strigoi!"

Nothing happened.

Fakeula smirked and let go of Tudor, who dropped to the deck, gasping for air. Fakeula approached me and lifted me up by my hair. I held onto his hand to lessen my scalp's pain as much as I could. My eyes welled with tears.

"One last time—what was in the jar, bitch?"

"Vlad's ashes!" I cried.

He let me go and I collapsed to the floor. Tears of frustration and fear poured from my eyes. I was defenseless, facing a vampire who could kill us both in an instant. Where was Mundibuto? "Mundibuto!" I screamed for help again.

"By the way," he said calmly over his shoulder, as he watched, with his arms folded, the vanishing luminous haze drifting up the hill. "I took care of the black vampire, Mundibuto. He will not come to your rescue, ever. And Strigoi do not work against vampires."

I gasped. We were helpless. And then I remembered my ampule with the vampire blue blood implanted behind my right ear. It contained a drop of Vlad's blood, and if I were in mortal danger, I could break the ampule, become contaminated, and evolve into a vampire. As a vampire, I had a fighting chance against him.

No, not really. If he had done something to Mundibuto, a hulk and a vampire, I was helpless—vampire or not.

He clasped his chin between his forefinger and thumb as if thinking, and after a while, he said, "Vlad's ashes. Hmm."

I nodded, crumpled on the floor.

"And he gave you specific instructions to spread his ashes from here?" He pointed around, while his cape flared out.

I nodded again, sobbing and tenderly touching my cheek.

"Did he tell you why he made that request? And don't lie, or I'll throw your boyfriend off the tower." He kicked Tudor.

I glanced worriedly at Tudor, who was on his knees, trying to catch his breath from the strangling and the kick. "No. He only told me he wished his ashes to lie where he was born."

"That sounds like Vlad V. But something tells me not to trust his innocent wish. That old vampire always had a trick up his sleeve."

I heard noises down below in the street. Beams of flashlights came from people calling my name. Dorin and Stanca were searching for me. I stood up and shouted over the railing, "Help!"

Only that one word came out of my mouth before I was yanked by my hair back from the railing. "You must have a death wish, bitch," Fakeula snarled through clenched teeth. "Nicolae, Ilie—come!" He called for the other two vampires, the traitors who had helped Vlad the Impaler's assassins.

Two shadows climbed over the railing. They came from outside the tower. One of them was the rough man I had met earlier, Nicolae. The other was the dandy in the white tuxedo and red bowtie I had spoken to at the Opera House and had seen in the lobby of the hotel in Timisoara.

"Nice to meet you, Cat. I'm Ilie," the dandy said pleasantly. He was dressed in a black tuxedo and black bowtie.

"Shut up, and let's take them in," said Fakeula.

Ilie pushed a rag into my mouth to silence me and wrapped a rope around my head to keep the gag in place. Another rough rope tied my hands and my ankles in front. He lifted me like a rolled blanket tied together at both ends and placed me on his left shoulder, my head hanging down. My blood drained to my head. To my horror, he climbed over the railing and descended down the wall. The street below was swinging under us. We were dangling in the air when he reached the beginning of the corbel arches, the outward projections that supported the upper part of the tower. I didn't dare look down so I looked up, as he held on to the downward-sloping corbel, one hand over the other, until he reached the tower's corner wall. I was so afraid that I even forgot to scream, though I was gagged. At the corner he scaled down the tower as if he were on a ladder until he reached the roof of the adjacent building. Nicolae came down after us, handling Tudor in the same fashion. Tudor's eyes bulged with horror, not knowing who or what these people were.

Despite my continuing fear of being dropped to the street below, they walked as easily and softly as cats on the roofs of the buildings. In a short time, we were off the roofs and climbing up the hill toward the church at the top. They didn't take us to the church, but to the cemetery, running with us on their shoulders among the marble-clad graves.

Near a brick wall, Fakeula moved a stone slab from the ground, and they took us down inside a catacomb, along dark corridors and stairways.

Chapter 12

We were dumped unceremoniously on the dirt floor. A torch on a wall came to life, and I saw Fakeula light a second one. I shook my head to get rid of the gag. Fakeula snapped his fingers, and Nicolae removed the gag and cut my ropes. He lifted me up into a standing position and, while holding me around my waist, he groped my breasts. I was not sure what offended me more: his groping or his putrid breath.

I turned my head and shouted, "Get your filthy hands off my breasts!"

"Nicolae, the little bitch is not yours to play with," admonished Fakeula. "She's a princess. Way below your station."

Nicolae let me go, reluctantly. Licking his lips, he whispered in my ear, "Such a shame not to taste you." Lightning-quick, he bit me on my neck. I felt two stings and then nothing as he sucked my blood. I resisted the narcotic in his saliva and hit him with my fists as hard as I could.

"What the hell did I tell you?" Fakeula pulled Nicolae off me and threw him against the nearest wall. "I want her intact. For now, anyway." He caressed my face with the back of his hand, sneering. I turned my head away.

"Who are you?" shouted Tudor after Ilie removed his gag and cut his ropes.

"They're vampires," I answered instead. The corners of my mouth hurt from the rope that had gagged me.

"Vampires! What vampires?" He was incredulous.

81

"Maybe this will shut him up," Ilie said as he moved toward Tudor. Ilie's eyes were bloodshot, and engorged blue veins pulsed on his neck and face. He opened his mouth wide, purple lips curling up. His inch-long, bone-yellow, vampire canines came out of their sheaths, dripping with gooey saliva, sharp, and ready to strike. A sound like that of a flushing toilet escaped from his throat.

At first Tudor bent back to escape the menacing mouth, but then he bent forward, examining Ilie as if he were examining a rare specimen. "I've never seen anything like this before." He even moved his head from side to side to take in all that he was seeing. That act may have surprised Ilie, as he followed Tudor's movement with his eyes.

Scientific curiosity aside, Tudor didn't know whom he was dealing with. The vampire could have ripped his head off with one bite. I ran in between them and pushed Tudor backward with my elbows. "That's enough, Ilie," I commanded him. Ilie seemed taken aback. I was a mere human, a mortal, giving him orders, but he obeyed. His canines retreated back into his mouth, his veins receded, and his eyes regained their usual color. I felt Tudor leaning over me, spellbound with curiosity at Ilie's transformation back to normal. I took Tudor by the elbow and pulled him away from Ilie.

Fakeula and Nicolae snickered at first but now they were quiet, uncertain of Ilie's submissive behavior, of the power I seemed to have over him. I didn't have any power over him, but I'd seen vampire faces just like his before. It didn't scare me any more, although the first time I saw it I peed myself. "Why did you bring us here?" I demanded to know.

"Why did we bring them here and not kill them?" Nicolae asked. His English seemed to have improved from that of the rough groundskeeper he had pretended to be at the cemetery.

"Shut up. You don't need to know. Just do as I tell you." Fakeula seemed irritated by his questioning.

"You dumb shit," Ilie said to Nicolae. "We brought them here so we can suck their blood without being bothered by the humans in the street."

"What do you mean, suck our blood?" Tudor seemed to finally understand. He asked them, "Are you hematophagous?"

"She told you what we are, and I showed you my face. We are vampires!" Ilie shouted.

"That's impossible. There are no vampires. You are just some mutation that needs medical help."

"They are mutations," I told Tudor. "And they are true vampires."

"No way," continued Tudor. "They'd have been discovered by now. They live here in Transylvania, in Romania, and Romania was a police state under communism. They would have known about them."

"What makes you think we were not communists back then?" Fakeula raised his eyebrows to make the point.

"And you drink blood and live forever?" Tudor asked.

"Nicolae and Ilie are over five centuries old," said Fakeula, nodding toward them. "And yes, we drink blood—yours, too, if you don't shut up."

Tudor stiffened.

"Stop asking questions," I whispered to him. "Let us go," I demanded from them.

"Nicolae, Ilie—put them in the cages," Fakeula ordered.

No sooner had he finished giving the order when the pair of vampires lowered two square and rusty wrought-iron cages by pulling on some chains. I gasped, not from seeing the medieval iron cages descend, but from seeing what else was hanging from the crypt's ceiling—hundreds of gray burlap sacks in the shape of bodies, suspended by ropes from around the ankles. It looked macabre. Human bodies, hung like hams from the ceiling. I felt bitter bile rise in my throat.

Fakeula caught my eye, and he looked up with a satisfied smile. "If you're lucky, you may not end up like them."

"What are those things?" Tudor asked hoarsely.

"What do you think they are?"

"They couldn't be human bodies." Tudor shook his head, not wanting to believe the obvious.

"Yes, they are bodies. Human, perhaps not." Fakeula began chuckling.

"Corpses?" he asked.

"Maybe. But that's not your concern," said Fakeula over the squeaking of the rusty chains as the cages descended. "We'll put you in those." He motioned with his thumb at the square cages.

They intended to keep us in those cages like animals. "Are you out of your mind? You cannot do that to us!" I screamed at him. He was watching the cage calmly.

Tudor took my hand and pulled me toward where he thought there was an exit. We ran as fast as we could in the dark until we came to a dead end. We had flashlights with us and turned them on, lighting a brick wall without any door or opening.

From behind us we heard screeching noises.

"Bats," said Tudor, searching with his light for any opening above us. "They may get entangled in our hair if they fly around."

I touched the top of my head and felt the creepy-crawlies run down my back at the thought of a flying rodent caught in my hair, shrieking and biting me. I pointed my light farther along to the ceiling. I couldn't believe what I saw. Tudor followed my stare.

On the ceiling, two creatures were crawling toward us. They were upside down on all fours and advanced as if they were crawling on the ground, defying gravity. The screeching noise came from their limbs clinging onto the stone ceiling. Their eyes shone red in our light beams, while they sneered devilishly at us.

They were Nicolae and Ilie.

"What in hell?" Tudor said in a shaky voice. Seeing a vampire with his fangs out was one thing, but seeing human shapes crawling on the ceiling like spiders was horrifying.

"You have nowhere to go," Fakeula said, approaching with a flaming torch in one hand.

We pointed our flashlight beams at him. He was walking on a narrow path, and something drew our attention to the floor. We froze.

Dozens of shiny black caskets packed the floor.

"Don't be afraid, Cat," said Tudor. "This is just part of the cemetery. We're in the catacombs, after all."

I knew better. This was a crypt for vampires.

Chapter 13

"Come, bitch," said Fakeula, curling his index finger back and forth at us. He turned around and walked back from where he came.

Nicolae and Ilie dropped from the ceiling onto their feet, silently, on either side of us. Their breaths, especially Nicolae's, were disgusting. There was no possible way to escape these vampires. I motioned to Tudor to follow Fakeula, so we wouldn't have to be vampire-handled again by these two.

"You seem to know these creatures," whispered Tudor.

"Yes, I do, but only the cosmopolitan types."

"What do they intend to do with us?"

"I have no idea." And I was as concerned as Tudor was about them. They knew I was the great-granddaughter of Vlad V Draculesti, and yet I had no sway over them. I was afraid for Mundibuto. What did they do to him? What would they do to us?

"What do you think is inside these?" Tudor pointed to the caskets as we walked by. "More vampires," he answered his own question.

"Not the vampires I know," I told him. The vampires I knew were civilized.

We returned back to the place we started from. The square iron cages were waiting for us just above the ground. Ilie and Nicolae unlatched the small iron doors on the cages and waited for orders from Fakeula. The cages swayed slightly.

On a wall nearby leaned a rake. Without hesitation, Tudor took it and pointed it at the vampires. "Get behind me, Cat." He moved the rake back and forth in a menacing way.

Except it was not menacing to the vampires. They looked at each other and laughed. In the blink of an eye, Fakeula stepped forward and pulled the rake out of Tudor's hands. Before Tudor could even react, Fakeula had grabbed him by the hair and sunk his teeth into Tudor's neck, sucking his blood. Tudor's body convulsed slightly, while Fakeula drank his blood for a full minute. Satisfied, the vampire stepped back and licked his lips.

Tudor stood on wobbly legs, confused as to what had happened. His blood pressure must have dropped considerably, and he fell to his knees before losing consciousness. I ran to his side and lifted his head. Slowly he awoke.

"What just happened?" he asked.

"You've just been bitten by a vampire, rake-man," Fakeula chuckled. The other two laughed, licking their lips as if expecting their turns.

"Don't touch him again," I pleaded. Those three could drink all his blood and kill poor Tudor. And I had involved him in this nightmare.

"Give me your bag and flashlights," he ordered us.

I gave him what he asked for. He put all my stuff in his pockets, throwing the empty bag back at me. I had no more use for it and I left it on the ground. Ilie emptied Tudor's pockets and gave everything to Fakeula.

"I'll leave the torches on," Fakeula said. "Other people before you have lost their minds when we left them here in the cages in total darkness. Pray that we return before the torches die out."

"Why don't you let us keep the flashlights?" Tudor asked.

Fakeula did not answer him. "Get inside the cages."

Tudor and I exchanged worried glances. If we did not climb in, Nicolae or Ilie would shove us in, brutally. I placed my right foot on the iron threshold and, bending down, I got in. I looked at the other cage, and Tudor was squeezing in through the small opening while Ilie was pushing him. Tudor sat in the cage. I stood up, holding onto the flat bars of the swinging cage, which had interlacing horizontal and vertical bars. Only my head might squeeze through the square openings. Nicolae and Ilie locked the doors with heavy, rusted padlocks and grinned at us.

"Lift them," Fakeula commanded the other two, and they pulled on the chains, lifting us eight feet off the ground. "Sit tight in there," he advised us. "Don't try anything foolish. I'll return after I figure out why you came to spread Vlad's ashes here in Sighisoara."

That was a good question. At one time or another I had wondered about that myself. But then Vlad V was born in Sighisoara, and it seemed like a reasonable request. Except for the date and the full moon—July 28 had a full moon. Why were the ashes to be spread during a full moon?

I looked at Tudor's cage, and when I looked down, the vampires were gone. In which direction did they go? Which way was the way out? And even if I had seen them leave, we were locked in iron cages, eight feet above the ground.

Tudor stood up in his cage, facing me. "Were those real vampires?"

"Yes, as real as they can get."

"How could this be? Dracula didn't exist before Bram Stoker wrote a fictional story about vampires."

"The vampires were around when he wrote the story," I said. "Who's to say that he knew more than he divulged? Maybe he met some of them?"

"But that would be a monumental discovery. How could he not let the world know about these creatures?"

"If I would have told you that vampires really existed before you encountered them, would you have believed me?"

"No, not without proof."

"Exactly. Bram Stoker did not have proof. The best he could do was to write a fictional story about vampires. He was lucky that they didn't kill him just because he wrote about them."

Chapter 14

"Cat, are you a vampire?"

"When we kissed, were my lips warm?"

"Yes, very warm and tender." His expression softened.

"Vampires are cold. In a way, they are like reptiles, and their temperature is the ambient temperature."

"How do you know so much about them? What's going on?"

I inhaled deeply. It was time to tell him some of the facts about vampires. "Tudor, I'm sorry I involved you in this."

He made a dismissive gesture.

"What I will tell you may shock you. Very few people, if any besides me, know about real vampires. I hope we'll get out of this, and when we do, for your own sake, I hope you will not divulge what you've experienced and what I will tell you. If you do, you will disappear."

"Disappear?"

"The vampires will kill you, and your body will never be found. The people who you'd tell about their existence would be killed as well. The vampires want to stay in the shadows, to stay a secret."

"I understand."

"Vampires are aware that once they were humans like you and me. By accident or other reasons, they were infected by the vampire strain and became vampires. They are not dead. They are quite alive. But their physiology is different. The ability of their bodies to heal and even seal their wounds without bleeding is superhuman. They are strong and quick."

"That's mind-boggling. Do they drink human blood?"

"Yes, they do. That's what gives them their incredible longevity."

"Was I bitten by them?"

"Yes, you were, by Fakeula. And I was bitten by Nicolae." I rubbed my neck, knowing that only two small purple dots were all that remained from the bite. "But don't be afraid—you and I will not turn into vampires. That's folklore."

"Why wouldn't we become vampires?"

"To become a vampire, your blood must be contaminated by their blue blood."

"I see—the pathogen is in their blue blood?"

"It is not blue blood like that which the nobility claims to have—their blood is red. The vampires have real blue blood. It is copper-based."

"Copper-based. My God. They're extraterrestrial aliens."

"They are human mutations, originally infected by aliens."

"That's unbelievable." He gave a whistle. "How did you get involved in this?"

"My great-great-great-grandfather was Vlad V Draculesti. He was a vampire, and he was the nephew of Vlad III Draculesti, Vlad the Impaler, also known as Dracula."

"No way!" Tudor shook his head. "You're not lying to me, are you?"

"No, I'm not lying to you." I smiled. "My great-grandfather was 560 years old when he died a couple of months ago."

"But vampires are not supposed to die."

"Yes, they do die. And also they can be killed, but not with silver knives or bullets or wooden stakes. And garlic is useless. I was with my great-grandfather in an Italian restaurant, and the garlic didn't bother him a bit."

"Then how can they be killed?"

"We won't be able to kill them."

Tudor did not ask any more questions about killing them, which was good. I wasn't about to tell him how a vampire could be killed. Yet.

"Why didn't Fakeula drink all my blood?"

"Well, the blood is not their nourishment. Human blood is the elixir of life for them. And they don't drink a lot of blood."

"That explains the absence of dead people, sucked dry of their blood. They drink only human blood?"

"They can drink animal blood as well, but it doesn't have the potency of human blood."

"If blood doesn't nourish them, what do they eat?"

"They don't eat. They drink. Alcohol."

"Alcohol? Yes, that makes sense. The alcohol is metabolized into sugar, and that's their sustenance."

I raised my shoulders. I didn't know the details of vampire metabolism.

"Were you bitten before?"

I nodded.

"By your great-grandfather?"

"No. Of course not," I said, disgusted. "He couldn't bite anymore."

"Since your great-grandfather was a vampire, how come you're not one of them? How old are you?"

"I am human, and I am 23 years old. My lineage goes back to Vlad V and his wife, Elena, and their daughter Anina. I resemble Elena, my great-great-great grandmother. That's how Vlad recognized me for who I was."

"Wow! How did Vlad become a vampire?"

"He and his uncle, Vlad the Impaler, became infected with the vampire strain while they were held hostage by King Corvinus. That's what Vlad told me."

"Vlad the Impaler was a vampire as well? But then how did they manage to kill him? You said they are hard to kill."

"His bodyguards Lazlo, Nicolae, and Ilie were the traitors who brought the Turkish assassins into the tent while Vlad the Impaler was asleep. They decapitated him."

"Nicolae and Ilie are the same people from back then?"

"Yes. Vlad the Impaler's blue blood contaminated Lazlo, Nicolae, and Ilie. They must have had open wounds, and that's how they got infected and became vampires. Lazlo was the leader, and Vlad V killed him later. Nicolae and Ilie hid from Vlad V and somehow they're still around."

"My God. This is incredible."

One of the torches flamed out. Filaments of smoke rose from the extinguished torch. Tudor and I looked at each other. Only one torch remained lit.

"What did he mean by going insane in the dark?" Tudor asked.

"I don't know. Something must happen in the dark." I shivered. The dim light of the remaining torch cast long shadows on the vaulted ceiling from the upside-down suspended bodies. All around our cages there were many of those burlap-wrapped bodies, some of them close enough to touch.

Tudor must have seen the fear in my face and asked, "Do you know what's in those sacks?"

"Fakeula said bodies."

"Yes, but in what state are those bodies, or, should I say, corpses?"

"What do you mean?"

"Are they mummies, or withered and desiccated bodies, or decaying corpses?"

"I think they are bodies. Fakeula would have said corpses."

"Bodies in suspended animation? Why?"

"An army?" I speculated, shrugging.

Tudor looked down below at the caskets. "Do you think there are bodies in those as well?"

I nodded. They wouldn't keep all these coffins empty. They housed something. More bodies.

"Fascinating. Some of them are in caskets, others in burlap sacks," commented Tudor. "Do you suppose there are vampires in the caskets? Sleeping or hibernating?"

"Vampires don't sleep in caskets." I tilted my head and pressed my lips together, thinking before I spoke. "Vampires are no different than us. They enjoy life, they have fun, and they even have sex. They do what we do. If they are in hibernation, it wouldn't be of their own free will."

"I suppose not. But then, who put them in there?"

"Fakeula and his cohorts," I answered.

"How many vampires are out there in the world?"

"Besides these three, there are three more who I know. Mundibuto, who stole your key, is a vampire."

"What happened to him? Why didn't he come to help you?"

"I'm afraid even to speculate. Mundibuto is built like a truck. But maybe three vampires are stronger than even Mundibuto."

The sack near me made a noise. Something was squirming inside. I shrunk from it.

"What's the matter?" Tudor asked.

"Something is moving in that sack." I pointed to it.

Tudor removed his belt. "Cat, catch my belt and let's pull our cages closer. We'll be farther from those things and closer to each other."

I extended my arms through the cage and at the second attempt I caught the belt. We both pulled on the belt until the cages touched. Tudor wrapped the belt around the cages' bars to keep them together. I took his hands. Mine were shaking. He kissed my hands to reassure me, but he was shaking, too.

And then the last torch went out.

Chapter 15

We were in total darkness. I uttered a short yelp. Tudor squeezed my hands to comfort me. I could hear his fast breathing. A small scratching noise came from behind my cage. I hoped that maybe it was a mouse.

"I wish my Strigoi could help us," I whimpered.

"What are you talking about? You've said that word before."

"They are my ghostly bodyguards. They couldn't help me against the vampires, but maybe they can come to the rescue now."

"Strigoi means 'ghosts' in Romanian. You mean you have ghosts that can protect you?"

"I know it is hard to believe," I said, trembling. "I inherited them from Vlad, and they've saved my life before."

"By now, I shouldn't doubt you about anything. Why don't you call them? Wait, what do they look like?"

"I don't think you'll be able to see them in this darkness. OK. Let me try." I released Tudor's hands, spread my arms, with my palms facing outward, and cried, "Strigoi! Help!"

Several white phantasms, like white smoke, materialized around our cages. They were white, not black as I remembered seeing them last time. Silently, they circled us slowly, flowing like ephemeral silk sheets.

"Are those Strigoi?" Tudor asked.

"Yes." They were finally here, but could they help us? I was neither in pain nor in any immediate danger. I concentrated and thought: *I need you to get us out of here.* There was no response from them. I had a feeling that they saw no threat against me. I squeezed my eyes shut, concentrating: *Break the locks.*

Incredibly, the lock on my door turned red, then yellow, then white. Bright light and heat emanated from the lock. It was melting.

"What's going on?" shouted Tudor.

There was enough light coming from the white-hot lock that I could see him. He was pointing to his cage's lock, which was melting as well. "I think they are heating the locks until the steel melts."

"We'd better kick at the doors," he said, and with a powerful kick that made his cage shudder and swing on its supporting chain, the iron door swung open. "Do the same!"

My cage, tied by Tudor's belt to his cage, was swinging as well. The padlock was white hot. Part of the iron door was getting red and hot. *Strigoi, break the door*, I mentally expressed the order. And the gate flew open, banging on the cage bars, and then it came back and closed again. I didn't wait. I kicked the door before the hot metal could cool down and lock me in again. The door swung open and stayed open.

"It worked!" shouted Tudor. "How did you do that?"

"Not me. My Strigoi." I watched as the padlock began to dim to a red hue, as the metal was cooling down. The flat bars behind me felt warm. The heat from the melting padlocks had warmed the rest of the cage.

"We have to wait until it cools down." Tudor touched the bars near the door opening and quickly pulled his hand back. There was hardly any light now coming from the dull red metal.

"Maybe I should ask them to lower the cages?" I proposed.

"What if they melt the chains and we drop down?"

"Maybe we should wait until the iron cools. I think we can jump down on our own."

"Yes. We'll have to hang from our hands before we drop. It's less distance that way."

"Agreed." Complete darkness returned. My Strigoi had come to the rescue once the vampires were gone. Then what was in the sacks and coffins? Perhaps not vampires.

"What's that?" Tudor asked.

I heard a ripping sound coming from the direction where I'd heard the small scratching sound before. I couldn't see anything, but something was making the noise of a cricket. Then it stopped.

The tearing sound continued. I held hands with Tudor. Whatever was out there, it could come into our cages. With the doors open, it could be as small as a rat or as big as one of us.

Another tearing sound came from behind Tudor. "I think something is ripping through the sacks." His voice sounded as if his head were turned toward the noise. There was more ripping, followed by more cricket noises, which soon became louder and metallic-sounding, as if a file were grinding against steel.

My cage suddenly swayed, as if something had just jumped onto it. "Tudor, I feel something on the outside of my cage." More metal grinding sounds enveloped us.

"Where?"

"Behind me. Wait, listen." Through the cacophony of metal grinding noises I heard something that made my blood run cold.

A screechy voice behind me said, "*Singe, singe, singe.*"

"What are they saying, Tudor?"

"Blood."

I felt a hand on my shoulder. Screaming hysterically, I reached and grabbed the arm. It was bony and leathery. I let go of Tudor's hands, yanked the thing off me, and ran to the opposite end of the cage. Two arms wrapped around my waist. I pulled off the bony fingers and moved away, still hearing, "*Singe, singe, singe,*" the call for blood.

Tudor howled, "What the hell are those things? Do they want blood? Call your Strigoi, Cat!"

"Strigoi!" I shouted. They did not appear, but there was a dim light coming from somewhere, which made matters even worst. We could see what was clinging on the outside of the cages—skeletal creatures with brown leathery skin dressed in rags. Deep black eyes in their skulls' eye sockets glowered lasciviously at us, while grayish-yellow, bony arms and hands were reaching inside for us. Their thin, brown lips were curling around their yellowed crooked teeth, anticipating our blood.

"Tudor!" I screamed while pushing those macabre limbs away from me.

"Did you call your Strigoi?" Tudor was fighting furiously to disentangle himself from the many arms that were keeping him pinned on the other side of his cage.

I looked up, enraged and ready to ask for their help again, and then I saw the source of the light.

Chapter 16

"Tudor, look up!" I screamed. Pushing those ghoulish limbs away from me, I stared, incredulous, at the blue light.

"Are those the Strigoi?" Looking up, Tudor finally freed himself.

Descending slowly from the ceiling was a bluish, luminescent haze. "It's Vlad's ashes," I said. The light became stronger as it descended.

"Stay near the common wall of our cages. They cannot reach us easily here. Luckily, they cannot bite us, either. The square openings of the bars are too small for their heads," said Tudor.

I moved closer to him, where his belt held the cages together, terrified by those fingers wriggling to reach me. I felt safe for a moment, but then I felt hands on my lower legs. I jumped and screamed.

"Stomp on them!" Tudor shouted, as he began jumping up and down and breaking finger bones.

I followed his advice and began smashing the fingers and even arms that were trying to grab me. Many of the creatures fell to the floor, unable to hold on to the cage's bars.

"What are these things?" Tudor asked.

I ventured a guess, "Zombies?"

Fingers grabbed my hair. They were on top of the cage now. I pulled myself free and ducked. It was best to semi-crouch, while occasionally stomping on a new intruder's fingers.

For a moment, I felt safe. They couldn't reach us from above with their hands, from below they got their bony fingers broken, and both of the cage doors were shut by the zombies, pressing in on one another. Brains were not their forte.

Through the gaps between their bodies, I could see the wild frenzy among the remaining zombies not on our cages. Some were dangling upside down, unable to free themselves from the ropes tying their ankles. Others were just coming out of their burlap sacks, like insects out of cocoons. Some were climbing up their ropes, but they stopped just below the blue cloud descending from the ceiling. Farther away, some of them had barely managed to punch their fingers through the burlap, while others were just squirming in their sacks.

We—or the scent of our blood—were awakening these zombies. The ones closer to us were already on our cages; the others were waiting their turn. I hoped that they would start fighting among themselves and give us a chance to escape, somehow. I wondered how fast they were and, if we jumped out of the cages, whether we could outrun them.

"Tudor, what if we jump out and run? There is enough light now."

I could see him looking around, assessing the situation, and breaking a zombie's fingers once in a while. "How do you suggest we get them to stand back and not swarm us?"

"How about if we take the belt off and let the two cages hang freely?"

"And then?"

"We can swing them and bash them together until we break the zombies or they fall off. They're only so many of them."

"There are hundreds of them," he said, looking around.

I stomped on another hand. This zombie fell down, and, surprisingly, it did not break. Instead, it stood up as if nothing had happened, staring up at the cages.

And then the horror of horrors took shape below us. Under the stronger light coming from the blue fog above us, I could see the casket lids being broken and smashed from within. Out of the coffins, vampires dressed in black sheepskin came out, their bloodshot eyes focused on us. Unlike the zombies, they were talking to each other.

"Cat," said Tudor, pounding on a new grabber, "what are those?"

"My guess is they are vampires."

"Can they reach us?"

I didn't want to answer him. Of course they could reach us. They could leap with no effort and enter our cages through the unlocked doors. I looked up, asking God for help. He was our only hope now.

The blue light from the haze was closer to the top of the cages. Everything around us was bathed in the blue light, making the bony yellow arms, fingers, and teeth look green, like mold on rotten food.

"Jeeesus!" I heard Tudor scream. A vampire was on the side of his cage, pulling off zombies and dropping them to the ground. But he wasn't saving Tudor; he was making room to reach the door and crawl inside.

"Close the door!" I shouted. But the door was already closed, from the zombies' bodies pressing in. My cage rocked. Another of the vampires had jumped onto it. He was heavier than a zombie, so the cages swayed more. He—no, she—was on the opposite side of the door and looked at me with bloodshot eyes. She opened her mouth sneering at me. She did not have the long canine teeth of a vampire.

These were worse than vampires. They were proto-vampires.

Chapter 17

"Tudor, these are proto-vampires!" I shouted to him, while he pulled at a zombie's arms to keep his door blocked. He looked at me, confused. "They are carnivores. They eat *flesh*."

Tudor exploded in laughter as another proto-vampire jumped onto his cage and tore at one of the zombies blocking the door. It made no difference what these creatures were: Vampire bloodsuckers or proto-vampire carnivores or zombies, we were as good as dead. A strong hand grabbed me by the ankle. I tried to shake it loose and stomp on it, but it was the hand of a proto-vampire.

What was I going to do now? Unlike the zombies, the proto-vampires were much stronger and quicker. I pulled with all my strength, but he reached with his other hand and grabbed me by the calf. I was pinned and couldn't move. However, he could not get into my cage either. It was a standoff.

And then a zombie hand clutched my other ankle. I pulled my foot away from this one, and luckily the proto-vampire holding my calf let it go to fight with the zombie crawling on his back. I managed to free my leg. The proto-vampire fell, but he landed on his feet and instantly jumped back onto the zombie under the cage, and both tumbled down. The proto-vampire tore the zombie in half, after which he jumped up and grabbed my ankle again. There was no way of escaping these beasts.

"Tudor!" I screamed. "A proto-vampire grabbed my ankle. I can't get loose!"

"Two of them have got both of my ankles, too!" He looked down. "They're fighting with each other." He tried to smile, hoping against hope.

We were finished for sure. I blew the hair off my face in frustration and despair, and looked up; the blue cloud was just above the cage. Creepy hands were reaching for me from above.

And then, something resembling gray sand began falling on me. What was that? I shook my head to get it out of my hair, but the sand continued to fall on me. "Tudor, are you getting sand in your cage?"

"Yes, what is this? Is the ceiling crumbling?"

Just as he said that, skeletal arms began falling on me and around me. Someone or something was tearing the arms off the zombies, letting them fall into the cage along with more sand. Creepy arms were strewn on the floor of my cage. Some of the fingers were still moving, as if to grasp my ankles.

It was raining sand. I tilted my head down to spare my eyes. If the floor of the cage had been solid, I might have been ankle-deep in sand. There was so much sand that the proto-vampire holding my ankle let go and fell to the ground. The sand must have gotten in his eyes.

And then the sand stopped falling. I shook my head vigorously to clear the piles of it that had fallen on my shoulders and hair. The top of the cage was clear of zombies, except for their raggedy clothes. The blue fog was below the cage's ceiling now. Whatever happened was beyond my comprehension. I couldn't see well above the blue dust haze, but below it the sand kept falling around the cages. I wondered if the sand came from the blue cloud?

Without the danger now of being yanked by the hair, I straightened up and was free to move about among the clutter of squirming bony arms. The zombies outside the cage's walls were still trying to grab me. Many other zombies were being pulled off by the proto-vampires, but as soon as one dropped off, another took its place from the dangling ropes nearby.

The blue blanket of fog descended and, to my astonishment, I finally understood the incredible phenomenon that was taking place. The blue haze was dissolving the zombies into sand. As the cloud descended and touched the tops of their heads, the solid skulls crumbled. I picked off a few grains of sand from my clothes and smelled them. They smelled burnt. This wasn't sand. These were ashes, the same ashes you get after cremating a corpse.

"Tudor, the blue cloud is cremating the zombies. Those are ashes, not sand!" I shouted over the noise made by the raining grains of ash.

Tudor was still struggling with a proto-vampire holding on to his leg. He looked up and around, and his mouth gaped in shock. "I'll be. How could this happen?"

"Vlad's ashes have made their way in here, and they're destroying the zombies." The blue cloud was a few inches above my head, and it was almost touching his head.

Tudor ducked down, afraid of the blue layer. "What is it going to do to us?"

"Nothing. It did not affect us when we were in the tower."

"Are you sure?"

I raised my left pinkie and cautiously touched the bottom of the cloud. My finger did not disintegrate. "It's safe." I stuck my whole hand through it. "It kills zombies, not humans."

"What will it do to the proto-vampires?" Tudor was pushing with his free foot to dislodge the hand holding him to the floor.

"I don't know. I haven't seen any of them exposed to it. Yet." I climbed up on the connected walls of our cages and stuck my head up above the blue layer. It was all clear. There was not a single zombie or proto-vampire above the blue blanket of haze. I came back down and looked outside to some of the sacks that were still occupied. As the blue cloud descended and engulfed the zombies' feet, it dissolved them. The rest of the bodies fell to the bottom of the sacks, squirming violently. As the cloud dropped down, it would leave behind just sacks with grainy ashes in them. There seemed to be hope for us after all. If only it would kill the proto-vampires as well.

My cage shook. The female proto-vampire had managed to come around the cage to the door side. She ripped the limbs off the nearby zombie. The other zombies hanging on the upper sides peeled off as they melted into ashes. Meanwhile, the female proto-vampire was struggling to open the door that was blocked by two more zombies. This was not good. She was definitely trying to get in and she knew how.

There weren't any new zombies jumping onto my cage. I didn't care about the remaining zombies around the other two sides of my cage. My worry was the side where the door was.

"I want your raw flesh!" she screamed at me in English and licked her lips.

Never, ever had I considered how prey might feel when cornered by a carnivore. I froze in total fear of what would happen once she was inside with me in the cage.

She pounded on a zombie at the door, and the zombie responded by clawing at her eyes. She shrieked and dropped down to the ground. Had the zombie won? Not for long, as another proto-vampire jumped to take her place and pulled that zombie's arm out of its socket. I looked around; several new proto-vampires were on the cage sides, pulling the zombies apart and discarding them. In a short time, only the proto-vampires would be left to reach for me.

The blue layer touched the top of my head. Tudor was still struggling with the menace below his cage. His cage had a lot more proto-vampires and very few zombies hanging on to it. Occasionally Tudor's head poked above the blue ceiling, but he would quickly duck below it to be able to see what was going on in his cage.

My cage rocked again. Another proto-vampire had jumped to near the door. The two of them tore the last zombie in half, and they began fighting with one another. That was good. They were punching and kicking each other, and they were ripping off some of the flat bars as if they were made of plastic. The fight was so intense that they forgot to hold on to the cage bars, and they both fell down. They continued fighting on the floor, splinters of wood flying from the broken caskets they were stomping on.

The menacing female proto-vampire jumped onto the door with new vigor. She sneered triumphantly. Only the iron bar door was between her and me. It was closed but not locked. I looked over my shoulder. The other proto-vampires were trying to grab me, just like the zombies had tried. "Hey!" I shouted. "She's alone at the gate. Don't you want a piece of me?" I ran close to the walls around the cage to entice them to follow me. It worked.

A new clump of proto-vampires was on top of the female, reaching in and trying to open the gate by pulling and pushing. The bitch was smart; she extricated herself from under them, climbed on top of them, and pushed all of them down. They fell in a heap. And then, with a quick move, she opened the gate and got inside, closing it behind her.

I was as good as devoured.

Chapter 18

She looked at me with hungry, red-rimmed eyes. She was drooling in anticipation of the blood and fresh meat that would satisfy her hunger.

It occurred to me that the safest place was to hang from the cage's top bars. If only I could reach them before she caught me.

She tensed as if getting ready to jump at me, but an arm reached from outside and held her back. She tried to free herself, and when she couldn't, she turned on her assailant and punched him in the face.

Enjoyable as the fight was to watch, I wasted no time and climbed to the ceiling along the joined sides of the cages. There was more than two feet of space above the blue layer. Partly crouched against one corner and partly hanging from the ceiling bars, I held myself above the layer. Would it work and protect me from the proto-vampires? I turned my head slowly and looked down. My darn hair hung down over my eyes and I had to flip it over my shoulder.

The punches and scratches she was getting from the outsiders bloodied the proto-vampire female. Two male proto-vampires locked their arms on each of hers. She straddled the doorframe with her legs and pulled away to free herself. Then suddenly she pushed out. The two outside lost their footing and let go of her arms to grab the bars of the cage to prevent their fall, but only one succeeded in clinging on. Two others replaced the one who fell, and the three of them began a new fight at the door entrance.

In the other cage, Tudor had managed to free his legs. Two proto-vampires were stuck in the door opening, neither one yielding to the other. Tudor was breathing heavily, exhausted by the effort of fighting off the zombies and the proto-vampires.

"Tudor, climb up to the ceiling!" I shouted to him.

At first he didn't seem to understand my instruction. One of the proto-vampires wormed his way in a little more and reached out to grab Tudor. In that instant, Tudor jumped and grabbed the upper bars, but a hand clutched one of his feet at the last second. He hung between the ceiling and the stretched arm of the proto-vampire. Stress showed on his face as he tried to hold on. As a last resort, he wriggled his foot out of his sneaker and pulled himself up to the ceiling, where he interlaced his feet in the bar openings, hanging above the blue layer.

"I pray we are safe here," I said. He dropped his head backward and we made eye contact. I could tell he was wishing that I was right.

"In case we don't make it, Cat, I'd like to tell you that it has been a pleasure to have known you. I wish we would have had more time together."

"We'll make it. I've managed to survive worse situations." I was lying. My previous mortal encounters were walks in the park compared to this, but I had to cheer him up. "And I feel the same way about you," I added and smiled at him. He gave me a broad, sad smile back.

The proto-vampires were causing a lot of commotion at the entrance to my cage. The three outside were all trying to squeeze through an opening only big enough for one. They were grunting and hissing and howling with madness. The female proto-vampire inside my cage was free to attack me, and we locked eyes—hers, victorious; mine, panicked. The blue layer was halfway down into the cage. It gave me some more freedom to loosen my position and relax my muscles.

She was cautious about the blue layer between her and me. It may have stopped her from jumping up to bring me down. Walking cautiously, half crouched, she tested the layer by poking a finger at it now and then, and retracting it quickly as if the haze had burned her. She looked confused, unable to figure out what that blue hazy thing was.

"Cat!" Tudor called to me. "The blue layer is going down faster now."

That was good news, and if it protected us, we would survive. Vlad's blue cloud of ashes had turned the zombies into coarse dust, but the effect it would have on the proto-vampires remained unknown. Down below on the ground, the zombies were fighting with the other proto-vampires. It was hard to say who was winning, although the zombies outnumbered the proto-vampires.

On Tudor's cage, the two proto-vampires were wedged in the door opening. Both of them had stopped fighting with each other and were just reaching out with their hands toward him. Tudor had more room as well above the layer, and he was able to assume a more relaxed position. He could have been hoping that the two vampires were stuck in the door for good.

The female proto-vampire dared to make a move. She reached out with both arms to grab me, but she screamed in agony, quickly withdrawing her smoking arms and blackened hands. The blue haze had burned her. She understood the danger, and for the first time I saw fear on her face. At the top of her lungs, she hollered at the three proto-vampires fighting at the doorway. She pointed to the blue layer and showed them her blackened hands.

"Tudor, did you understand what she said?" I asked him.

"Yes. She spoke in Hungarian, and she told them that the blue layer had burned her. But the other three in the doorway must be Romanians, because they didn't understand her."

It was true: After a brief pause, they recommenced punching each other to get in. The female hurled herself against them, trying to get out. She was shrieking and pounding on them, but to no avail. The other three were trying to get in and were not budging.

"I think that my two assailants in the door speak Hungarian and understood what she said." Tudor pointed to the pair, who now were trying to get out. Unfortunately, they were like a cork in the doorway and, without a lot of cooperation, they were stuck.

The female proto-vampire was exhausted from her efforts to get out. In desperation, pushing with her heels, she scurried backward into a corner. She stayed there, watching fearfully as the blue layer came closer to her.

To my amazement, she crouched into a jumping position and launched herself toward me.

Chapter 19

My eyes were wide with fear. She was trying to penetrate the layer and get at me. As if in slow motion, I saw her coming toward me, arms outstretched, fingers like claws, eyes blazing. Her whole body penetrated the blue layer in a flash, but instead of grabbing me, she grabbed on to the ceiling bars and raised her feet above the layer, just like me.

Oh, my God! She had made it above the last protection I had. I dropped to the floor to get away from her.

And then she exploded in a ball of fire, still hanging from the ceiling.

Quickly, I climbed back up into a safe ceiling corner, while shielding my face with one arm from the hot flames.

Her legs unfolded slowly while her hands were locked on the bars. Not only were her clothes burning, but her body was as well. The stench of burned flesh was noxious. Sizzling and popping sounds erupted from her body, and finally her fingers tore off and her body dropped down to the cage's floor.

As she passed through the blue layer, the flames died down, but her body glowed like embers. It looked as if she were a wooden statue glowing red, with a thin layer of ashes forming on the outside.

"Tu-Tu-Tudor! D-d-did you see t-t-that?" I pointed to the body, slowly disintegrating into hot ashes.

"I saw it!" he exclaimed, his eyes practically bulging out of his head.

No sooner had we exchanged those words when the blue layer descended on the proto-vampires stuck in the door. They went up in flames. Every proto-vampire not touched by the blue haze dropped down from the cage. Tudor and I found refuge at the sides opposite the doors, covering our mouths and faces with the fronts of our shirts. Slowly, the burned bodies in the doors dropped in pieces onto the floor, exploding in sparks like burning logs.

The blue layer was now below the cage, and down below there was hell. The zombies did not understand the danger and were reaching for the proto-vampires for their blood. The proto-vampires understood the peril and were running around in circles, trying to find an escape while occasionally tearing a zombie apart.

The hall of the catacomb was a large rectangular space with a vaulted ceiling. There hadn't been an exit in the direction we had run in earlier. However, now I saw that there was an exit at the opposite end, up some stone steps. The blue layer was halfway down the stairs, trapping the zombies and proto-vampires alike.

"All of them will burn," I told Tudor.

He nodded grimly. "Goddamn it," he cursed. "We survived these monsters tearing us apart, but we will die from smoke inhalation or be cooked."

Tragically, that was true. It was warm from the three proto-vampires burning, but once the blue layer reached the floor, everyone down below would ignite and burn in hot flames. And we would be barbecue meat up in the cages. We couldn't remain in the cages; we had to get out to save our lives. Dropping down to the floor would be like jumping back into the fray and being quickly killed. But if we stayed up here, we were going to be roasted alive.

I looked toward the entrance of the crypt. How to get there? From our cages to the exit, there was a forest of hanging ropes left from the burlap zombie sacks. "Tudor, maybe we can swing on the ropes to reach the stairs," I proposed.

He looked at the hanging ropes. "That seems to be the only way. Can you swing on those ropes to get there?" He pointed to the exit.

"I'll have to. Can you?"

He gave me a but-of-course look.

"OK, Tarzan."

"Did you know that Johnny Weissmuller, who played Tarzan in the movies, was born in Timisoara, my city?"

A little detail that I didn't need to know at the moment, unless he was trying to defuse the tension of our dire situation. "In that case, I won't have to worry about you," I smirked. He shook his head in amusement.

I kicked at the pile of hot ashes remaining from the proto-vampire, and they fell down through the floor bars. To get out of the cage, I lay on my back in front of the door opening and scooted myself out headfirst, grabbing the bars above the door and pulling myself up and out of the cage. I got on top of the cage at about the same time as Tudor, and he jumped to my cage to join me. He managed to put his lost sneaker back on and recovered his belt. I needed a hug, and he took me into his strong arms. We were alive.

"We have to move," he said into my ear. "Me Tarzan, you Jane."

That made me smile. And without saying another word, he jumped toward the nearest rope, six feet away. My heart was in my throat. He caught the rope, swung away and then swung back. He landed on the cage with the rope in his hand.

"W-w-wow," I couldn't restrain my disbelief and admiration for what he'd done. "Where did you learn to do that?"

"I was a gymnast when I was a kid, but I grew too big to continue in that sport. Are you sure you can do this?"

I nodded. How difficult could it be?

"Now, remember, you should always have your hand on a rope. Some ropes are closer to each other, some are farther apart. As you swing away, aim for a rope, then let one hand go and grab it, and then let go of the previous rope. You will not be able to swing from rope to rope like me. Or Tarzan. After you grab the next rope, swing backward with it, and then aim for the next one. Don't lose momentum—you must keep swinging. Are you sure you can do this?" he asked me again.

"Yes, I can. I have to." I gave him a small peck on his dusty cheek. "See you at the other end, Tarzan." I held the rope with both hands, stepped back a few paces, and aimed for a rope in the distance. I ran and became airborne.

What was I thinking? I wasn't Nadia Comăneci. My arms felt as if they were coming out of their sockets. I lost my concentration and my aim, and I closed my eyes. A rope hit me in the face, but I didn't let go of the rope I was hanging on and I swung back to the cage, where Tudor caught me.

"Hang in there. I'll push you," Tudor said, and he gave me a shove.

With my eyes open this time, I flew between several ropes, too fast to be able to grab any of them. Then I saw one rope approaching slowly, as if in a dream. This was the rope I would grab. My right hand reached out and locked on to the new rope. I let go of the old rope. But I couldn't hold on to the new one for long; I began sliding down the rope, my hand burning from the friction. I desperately grabbed it with the other hand. But my right palm was hurting so bad that I let go of the rope. My left hand couldn't hold me and I began to slide down again, now getting friction burns on the left palm.

I couldn't stand the pain and let go of the rope. I fell.

Chapter 20

"Caaat!" I heard Tudor yell after me.

From a height of about eight feet or more, penetrating the blue layer, I landed on my butt on top of a zombie. It felt as if I had hit a bundle of twigs that cracked and shattered. The zombie, squirming on the floor under me, had softened my landing, sparing me any broken bones. My unexpected crash cleared a circle around me, and I stood up, breathing hard.

"Cat, are you OK?" shouted Tudor. He looked as if he were ready to jump after me.

"I'm fine. Stay where you are!" I looked around. Zombies and proto-vampires began noticing me. Their bloodshot eyes locked on me, and slowly they began approaching.

I looked up for the blue layer. It was about two feet above me and would not descend fast enough to make a difference. The stairs were at least 50 feet away, and in between them and me stood dozens of monsters. What an awful way to die. I shuddered, disgusted by the macabre scene around me. Reaching arms with clawed hands approached me, shuffling on the grainy ashes that covered the floor.

The zombies were slower than the proto-vampires, and one part of the circle surrounding me was thick with them. Without hesitation, I ran and rammed into them like a football player, head-on. Fortunately, my head squeezed between two zombies and my shoulders pushed them aside. Then my head smashed into the belly of another

125

zombie. It felt as if I had hit a sack of sand, definitely harder than flesh. I had enough momentum and didn't bounce back, but fell face down on top of the zombie. My head ached.

This was no time for pleasantries or pardons. I struggled back to my feet and ran, trying to find my way through them to reach the stairs. It didn't work; I was corralled with my back against the wall. The proto-vampires began shoving the zombies aside. The zombies resisted and fought back, but lost. Many of the proto-vampires were festooned with dismembered arms with hands and fingers clinging to their sheepskin clothes, their arms, and even their necks. The ripped-off limbs kept squirming.

My back was against the wall, and I felt a jagged edge. I grabbed whatever it was and pulled out a good-sized plank, which was ripped from a coffin. Holding it with both hands, I used it as a spear to keep the monsters at a distance. They kept getting closer. Some proto-vampires laughed sinisterly at my attempt to defend myself.

With a crashing bang, Tudor landed just behind the front attackers and knocked them down, like pins being hit by a bowling ball. He had swung down on the ropes and was coming to my rescue, except the proto-vampires saw him as an additional treat, not a threat. He propped himself in front of me, took the plank from me, and, using it like a spear, he charged forward. I followed, but both of us fell to the ground after we stumbled on a broken casket. We rolled onto our backs, and a circle of monsters towered over us. It was inevitable—we were going to be pulled apart, limb from limb.

Chapter 21

"Cat," Tudor said calmly. "Do you think that you can summon your Strigoi?"

In the heat of the action and discouraged by their unreliability, I had forgotten about my Strigoi, but I wasn't sure if they would come to my rescue.

I got up, knees bent, and extended my arms, palms out. Without calling for them, I imagined the circle made by the monsters being pushed out.

As if they were blown back by a strong wave of invisible power, the monsters fell backward. It worked. I put my hands together, arms extended toward the stairs, and then separated them, palms out, as if parting the Red Sea. A clear path formed from us to the stairs, while the monsters were blasted backward.

"Let's run for it!" I straightened up, grabbed Tudor by the hand, and together we ran to the stairs. We climbed fast to get above the blue layer, and then we stopped to catch our breath and cough up the dust from our throats.

The proto-vampires and zombies got up, saw us, and approached the stairs. They were relentless.

"Why didn't you use your Strigoi to get to the stairs before trying the ropes?" Tudor asked.

"I forgot about them."

"Don't they come to your rescue when you're in danger?"

"That's what I thought. I don't know much about them and how to use them. I'm in training." And I was. This last time I didn't ask for them, but I used their power by simply visualizing the action that needed to be taken. Maybe this was what I had to do all along. In a way, I had done exactly that when I killed the vampire slayers back at the Silver Coffin Nightclub in New York, but I did not realize it at the time.

"Do you think you can use them against the vampires now?" Tudor asked.

I shook my head. "Not against them. We are on our own when we deal with them."

Tudor rubbed the back of his neck. "We're in deep trouble," he said softly.

Any words of encouragement or hope would be a lie. We had managed to escape from the imminent danger of the zombies and proto-vampires, but the vampires would catch and kill us. I looked at the blue haze below us, only six feet above the floor and resembling a layer of blue cigarette smoke in a tavern. I didn't want to imagine the inferno that would soon follow.

Tudor took me by the hand and pulled me a few steps higher. The crowd below was getting restless, and they were herding at the bottom of the stone steps. The proto-vampires were up front and the zombies were behind, pushing in to climb the stairs. The zombies were calling again for blood, "Singe, singe, sinege...."

The proto-vampires, who weren't aware of what had happened to their three brethren, tested the blue layer and got their fingers burned. They got the message. I wasn't sure if they understood that they would all die. They spoke to each other in huffy and irritated tones.

"What are they saying, Tudor?"

"They are afraid and hungry. They don't understand what is going on. Some are debating whether to jump through the layer, and others don't want to take the risk."

"What languages are they speaking?"

"Romanian, Hungarian, German, Serbian, and a bunch of other Slavic languages. Even Gypsy."

"European languages."

"Mostly Central European languages. Yes, this seems to be a localized abnormality."

"Abnormality?" I wondered.

"Well, what do you call this?" Tudor motioned toward the monsters below, who kept pushing but were unable to advance. "Whatever transformed these people into what they are today is bad news. I wonder if it is contagious."

"I know how the proto-vampires came to be." Tudor turned his head quickly toward me. "I was told of one such incident. But I have no idea how the zombies were made."

"I hope the blue layer destroys all the contagious elements down there." His demeanor darkened. "We may have been infected as well. Do you have any open wounds?"

He and I rolled up our sleeves and then checked our ankles and calves.

"I don't have any open wounds. But you do." Tudor looked at my right cheek.

Yes, Fakeula had reopened my wound when he had slapped me. I put my hand on my cheek, touching it tenderly. Like any good doctor, Tudor pulled an adhesive bandage from one of his back pockets and applied it to my wound.

"We're not contaminated," he said with assurance. "The blue haze probably destroys such pathogens, and we went through it several times, including just now."

I nodded. Sounded good to me. He was the doctor.

Down below, the commotion grew. The blue layer was lower now, and the zombies encircled the proto-vampires in the front pushing them closer and closer to the blue death. Some proto-vampires began pushing back, but they couldn't break through and run away. A few others on the front line, stubbornly, kept testing the blue layer.

With a howl, two proto-vampires ran up through the deadly layer. They burst into flames, collapsed, and rolled back down the stairs, landing in front of the others like two logs of red embers.

They finally understood that there was no way through. The front line of proto-vampires turned around and pushed to get away from their burning comrades. The zombies became excited and pushed forward even harder. Chaos erupted; it was every monster for himself. The zombies pushed from behind so hard that soon several proto-vampires were shoved up into the blue layer, igniting instantly.

The compact group of monsters broke apart as the frantic proto-vampires broke through the zombies with desperate might. They ran away from the stairs. Some zombies followed them, but others advanced toward us, toward their disintegration. They moved slowly up the stairs and, as each one poked his head through the blue layer, each began dissolving into ashes.

Headless zombies pushed ahead, followed by more of them. In a matter of minutes, they were all a pile of ashes and bones and rags at the bottom of the stairs. The blue layer was now a few feet above the ground, and the remaining standing zombies were turned into flowing sand. They stood like statues as the blue layer consumed them. Some even continued walking, first without their heads, then without their upper torsos, until they turned completely into ashes.

The proto-vampires took refuge in their caskets, lying down in them as if taking shelter. I began to feel sorry for them. The zombies were the walking dead, but the proto-vampires were alive and afraid to die. I heard voices from each coffin. Each one was praying in his or her own language and Christian religion, awaiting death.

Chapter 22

I covered my face, and Tudor took me in his arms. "We'd better get out of here," he said. He was right. Soon this entire hall would become an inferno. Tudor took me by the hand, and I followed him up the twisting steps.

The stairs forked in different directions, into other tunnels. Tudor was searching for a way up and out. We walked in darkness until we arrived in a spot that was illuminated by a beam of light from above. It was a ventilation shaft. At a T-ending, we took the right corridor for no particular reason. Luck was with us, and soon we were climbing through a small opening into a mausoleum chamber.

It was a high-ceilinged room, with barred openings at the top for air and light. At the bottom, where we had entered, there were marble burial boxes, but higher up, the coffins were made of heavy wood in various stages of deterioration. It smelled of earth and decay. We climbed up to the atrium at the ground floor, which had a few stone benches, statues of angels, and urns. There weren't any flowers in the urns. The place has not been visited in a while.

A heavy black double-door was between us and the fresh air and daylight outside. Tudor tried to open the door but couldn't. "It's locked from the outside with a chain," he said, pushing against it.

"Stand back, Tudor." I shoved my open hands toward the door and it burst open. The power I possessed was unbelievable, and I was mastering it fast.

Tudor did not hesitate and pulled me out by the hand. We went down a few steps and found ourselves in the cemetery. We came out of the Greco-Roman-style mausoleum with the black colonnades. The double doors were intact, but the heavy chain and padlocked latches were ripped off the wood.

"Tudor, we need to shut the doors so they don't attract attention." He and I climbed back up and closed the double doors, which stayed closed, fortunately.

We walked along the graveyard trail until we spotted a policeman at the entrance of the cemetery. Cautiously, I steered Tudor away to the left to find another exit.

"Why are we avoiding the policeman?" Tudor asked.

Half-crouched to stay hidden behind the rectangular headstones and crosses, I replied, "Why do you think he's there?"

"Looking for you."

"Well, I don't want to be found."

"Why not?"

"They'll want explanations, and we haven't agreed on a common story yet," I said.

Tudor straightened up and put his hands on his hips, but reconsidering, he shrugged and followed me. We walked off the cemetery's flat grounds where there was no fence and descended through a wooded area toward the Gothic church. We walked casually on a path toward the covered walkway that had led us up here. There were other policemen around, and two were guarding the entrance to the downhill path. There was no way down without being spotted.

Near the church, a narrow two-story house stood at the edge of the slope. We moved closer to it, trying to see if we could find another path back to town.

Tudor looked at me. "You and I look as if we've been through hell."

"We were, wouldn't you say?" I looked at him. His face was marked with black soot. I imagined I looked the same. And my hair must have been a mess. My clothes were black but were streaked by the dust and ashes that had settled on them. Tudor had on a shirt that was once gray and now resembled a rag used to clean a chimney.

He motioned with his head and walked to the house, where he knocked on the door. No one answered. Boldly, he pushed down on the handle and the door opened. "*Buna ziua. Cineva acasa?*" he called out. "Hello?" He stepped inside and motioned to me to follow.

He closed the door after me. "What are you doing?" I whispered, looking around. We were in a room that served as the kitchen, dining room, and living room all in one. A set of wooden stairs led to the upper level and another steeper staircase descended below.

He walked to the kitchen sink and turned the brass faucet handle, the water pouring into a round galvanized-metal basin. "At least we can wash our faces and hands." Without another word, he began soaping and then rinsing his hands and face. At least his face was relatively clean again. "Come on," he invited me. "Careful, there's only cold water."

Shaking my head in disbelief at what we were doing, I went to the sink and washed my face and hands. I felt better. "Whose house is this?"

"Probably the church's groundskeeper and his family." Tudor looked outside through the glass panes of the door. "Dorin and Stanca must be nearby."

"Do you think they saw us?"

He shook his head. "We cannot get out until they leave." He looked out again. "They brought search dogs."

What else?

"Maybe they have a backdoor down there." He pointed down the steep stairs and descended to a lower level. A moment later, his head popped back up. "There is a way out."

On my way to the stairs, I passed a table and noticed pepper and saltshakers. I took the peppershaker and covered the area in front of the door and the path to the stairs with pepper.

"Why did you do that?" he asked.

"It may throw off the dogs, if they find our trail here."

He looked at me, perplexed, as if wondering how I knew how to cover our tracks.

"I saw it in a movie," I explained.

We climbed down into a narrow room that served as a cellar. A glass-paned door led out the back of the house, and we exited on a landing at the bottom of the house on the hill's downslope. A footpath zigzagged toward the town's orange clay tile roofs below.

We chose to enter Tudor's hotel through a back-alley entrance, because a policeman was posted at the front door. Quietly, Tudor went to the front desk, which had no one there, and removed his key from the hook. Just as quietly, we took the stairs to his room. No one was there in front of the door. Once inside, I placed my arms around his neck and laid my head on his chest, momentarily relieved that we had found a safe haven.

"Do you want to take a shower?" He motioned with his head toward the bathroom.

"I definitely want to wash the death from my hair and skin." I walked to the bathroom, removing my shirt, then stopped, turned around, and asked, "Do you want to join me?"

He didn't wait for a second invitation. He took off his sneakers, discarded his clothes, and joined me in the shower. There was room enough for both of us, and the warm water felt good cascading over us. I shampooed my hair and lathered my body, and Tudor soaped my back. I reciprocated. His body was nice, trim, and smooth. Cute buns, too. And I couldn't help but glance at his manhood. Healthy.

There were enough towels for both of my hair, and us but instead of drying thoroughly, we ended up avidly embracing and kissing. Tudor lifted me up in his strong arms and took me to his bed.

And we made passionate love.

Chapter 23

We slept, exhausted from our ordeal and our lovemaking. I woke up and looked through the window. Dusk was upon Sighisoara. Next to me Tudor was sound asleep.

Sitting up against the headboard, I assessed what had happened. I had come to Transylvania, to Sighisoara, to spread Vlad's ashes from the Clock Tower at midnight during a full moon. Originally, I thought that the exact spot, time, and moon phase were Vlad's whim. It was not. He knew about the zombies and the proto-vampires and how they could be destroyed. How could his ashes decimate those monsters so thoroughly? Maybe it was the combination of the full moon and the date.

And me.

Actually, not me, but the Strigoi—that's what destroyed them all.

Using Vlad's ashes, they were the ones who turned those monsters into dust. And as far as spreading the ashes from the Clock Tower, Vlad may not have known the exact location of the monsters, but he knew they were in Sighisoara. The tower provided the wide viewing range to find them.

Who created the monsters? Fakeula, Ilie, and Nicolae? Why? For whatever sick plans they had in mind to take so many lives and change them into monsters. Where were they now? And what would they do when they found ashes instead of monsters?

Tudor rolled over but stayed asleep. I had made a big mistake involving him in this affair. I was endangering his life—I had to leave him.

Quietly, I gathered my smelly clothes, got dressed, and left him sleeping.

Outside the hotel all was quiet, and there were no cops. It was early evening, and people were having drinks and dinner in the open-air cafes in the street. At one café, seated at a table against the wall and having a drink of *palinca*, was a large and muscular black man. It was Mundibuto.

We made eye contact. He extended a hand and invited me to sit down.

"What happened?" we both asked at the same time.

"You first," he said.

"No, you first." I grabbed two soft buns from a basket in the middle of the table and stuffed one into my mouth. I was so hungry.

"You stink," he said, skewing his face.

I rolled my eyes, knowing full well that I smelled acrid and needed to change my clothes, like, immediately.

"We cannot talk here." He stood up and dropped a ten-euro note on the table.

Stuffing the other bun into my mouth, I grabbed two more and followed him down the street. We ended up near another church at the other end of Sighisoara. The door was open, and we sat in a back pew.

"Where were you?" I asked him impatiently.

"I was ambushed by Nicolae, Ilie, and the other vampire that looks like Vlad," said Mundibuto.

"How could that happen?"

"It has never happened before. But this time I was distracted by the blue cloud above."

"Vlad's ashes," I clarified.

"That's what it was? Anyway, while staring up, the three of them grabbed me, immobilized me, and threw me into a deep stone shaft, in the crypt of the church near the Clock Tower."

"Goddamn it!" I couldn't help taking His name in vain. "How did you manage to get out?"

"That's why they threw me in there. The shaft was carved in limestone, and they blocked the entrance to the shaft with a large stone slab. I didn't have enough leverage to push the slab off, and I could have been left there to die. Luckily, near the entrance I found a crack and I managed to enlarge it and squeeze my way out of there. It took me until this morning.

"I checked for you at your inn and at Tudor's hotel, and then the situation became complicated when the secret agents brought the police to search for you. I didn't know where you were. I posted myself at a table in town to be seen by the three vampires and to search from there. And then there you were."

"How did they know about me coming here?"

Mundibuto shrugged. "Somehow they knew about you and had planned ahead, including how to deal with me."

"The first time I'd seen Ilie and Fakeula was in Timisoara. They followed me all the way here. What are we going to do, Mundibuto?"

"I'm going to kill them," he said matter-of-factly. "Fakeula? Is that what you call him?"

I nodded, and one side of his face bent up in a smile.

"But there are three of them, Mundibuto."

"As I said, they took me by surprise. But they are as good as dead." He was determined. "I gather they kidnapped you and your friend, Tudor. What happened?"

"Oh, not much."

Mundibuto raised an eyebrow.

"They took us to hell." I told him the whole story.

He was stunned by what he heard. "Proto-vampires and zombies. Vlad's ashes destroyed them," he said pensively. "Or, as you think, the Strigoi."

"Who could have created that army?" I wondered. "And why keep them down there, as if in hibernation?"

"Zombies and proto-vampires need to be nourished. Not to mention that, if they're awake, they might be difficult to control. And they'd age."

"Age?"

"I'm not sure about the zombies, but the protos age and eventually die. If kept in hibernation, as you said, they can be awakened when needed."

"Needed for what?" I felt a chill run down my spine.

"The three vampires will tell us. Before they die."

144

"When they find only ashes, they'll go ballistic. What do we do now?"

Mundibuto sniffed the air. "Presently, they're not around. I may need you to bait them." He looked at me intently.

I inhaled apprehensively. Those three vampires would not go away, and even if I got back to the States, they'd come after me, thirsty for revenge. Mundibuto was right. I had to go back into the catacombs. They had to die.

Chapter 24

"What do you want me to do?"

"You need to go back where they left you."

"When?"

"Right now. And keep those clothes on. That will make them less suspicious."

"And you?"

"I'll be in there. Prepared." He opened his wide vest. I saw two Uzis holstered under his arms.

"Firepower?" I furrowed my eyebrows, unconvinced of their effectiveness.

"That's to disable them. I'll behead them to finish the job."

"OK. But as you found out, my Strigoi will not touch them."

"No, they will not take offensive action against them, but they'll help you take evasive actions," he said.

"What do you mean?" That intrigued me.

"Don't call your Strigoi to attack them. Ask them to help you stay away from them. Don't let the vampires catch you."

"Ahh! Got it. One more thing—I want Tudor left out of this."

"Definitely. He could be a handicap." He was right, and I didn't want any more harm to come to Tudor.

"By the way, I saw them walk on the ceiling," I said.

"Yes, and?"

"Can you walk on the ceiling?"

"Sure."

"How do you do that?"

"You'd have to be a vampire to understand." He grinned.

I left it at that.

"Ready?" he asked.

"Let's go get rid of them."

To approach as stealthily as we could and avoid any detection by the police, in case they were still around, I climbed onto Mundibuto's back, and soon we were at the mausoleum's entrance. Along the way, he picked up a heavy leather handbag. He gave me several pen-size flashlights, which I stuffed into my pockets and one in my bra, in my cleavage. From the bag he pulled out two double-blade medieval axes, which he placed crisscrossed on his back.

"And here is a bottle of water and a sausage sandwich." He handed me the bottle and my meal. Mundibuto was a caring vampire.

We got inside, and I took him down through the tunnels to the crypt where we'd faced extinction. He had a big flashlight and—more for my benefit than his, because he could see in the dark—he turned it on. Compared to what used to be there, the hall looked dead, dusty, and peaceful. The coarse ashes of the zombies were spread all over, covering the bottom of the stairs and the floors in a thick layer. Larger bones occasionally stuck up like twigs through sand. Where the caskets had been were piles of fine dust in the shape of the corpses inside them. Those were the proto-vampires' remains.

"Good job." Mundibuto gave a short chuckle. "What in hell were they planning here?" He shook his head.

"No one could imagine what once lived down here." I was stupefied at the site below us.

"OK, Cat. I'll have to get you up there in one of the cages."

The two cages hung lazily among the ropes. "The nearest cage was mine."

He motioned to follow him down the stairs. At the bottom we walked on the thick layer of coarse ashes that felt like kitty litter under our feet.

"I'll throw you up there." He motioned to the cage.

"How about if you just lift me? I've discovered that I'm not an acrobat."

With ease he lifted me onto his shoulders. The bottom of the cage was at waist level, so I crawled inside without much difficulty. Below me, I saw Mundibuto turn suddenly and stare at the top of the stairs. I turned one of my flashlights on and pointed it in that direction.

Tudor stood at the top of the stairs.

"What are you doing here?" I screamed, afraid for his safety.

"I could ask you the same question," he answered.

"Tudor, I don't want you to get hurt. Go back."

"And I don't want you to get hurt. I came to protect you."

Mundibuto snickered.

"What's so funny?" Tudor demanded.

"You, of course. How are you going to protect Cat against three vampires?"

"And who's going to protect her? You? Where were you when we needed you?"

"Tudor, stay out of this," I said. "Please go back."

Tudor looked around the room. "I see you're setting a trap, and Cat is the bait."

"Very intuitive of you," snarled Mundibuto.

"As you may recall, I was in the other cage."

"Your point?" Mundibuto asked. "Wait, I see—you want to get into the other cage?"

"Something like that."

"No, Tudor! Please leave!" I yelled at him from my cage. I was petrified. I didn't want anything to happen to him.

"Cat, that's a better plan," said Mundibuto. "They will not suspect anything if each of you are in your cages. Come on down, hero, and make sure you roll around in the ashes."

Tudor came down the stairs. "Why do you want me to roll in the ashes?"

"I'm sure you don't know about this, but vampires have a keen sense of smell. You don't want them to smell your fresh-as-a-breeze deodorant."

Tudor did not comment and knelt down in the ashes. He even placed a handful on his head and rubbed his face with the dust. He extended a hand to Mundibuto. "Hello, we haven't properly been introduced earlier. I'm Dr. Tudor Lupu."

"Nice to meet you, Doctor. I'm Mundibuto." They shook hands, and Mundibuto inspected him. "Excellent. I'll do the same." He rubbed himself with the ashes and poured shovel-sized handfuls onto his shiny bald head. "Now we all are one with the crypt." With a quick motion, he threw handfuls of ashes at me to disguise my freshly shampooed hair and showered body.

Tudor was lifted to the cage, and he climbed in. "You two will have to share the sandwich and water. I only brought one."

"Are you hungry?" I asked Tudor.

"Yes, but I'm afraid if I eat I may throw up when I witness what may happen here. But thanks."

"Are you good up there?" Mundibuto asked.

We nodded and closed the doors to the cages.

"Please, no lights. They left you in the dark, and you must stay that way. You can talk if you want, but you'll not hear from me from now on. Only after they arrive."

"Wait," I said. "Let me give Tudor one of the flashlights, just in case."

"OK. And don't talk about me." Mundibuto turned off his flashlight, and we were plunged into total darkness.

Chapter 25

I sat down and crossed my legs. There was no reason to keep my eyes open in the darkness, and I closed them. The air smelled like ash and dust, and my scalp itched from the dirt. I concentrated on my hearing, and soon I could hear Tudor's breathing. Whatever was about to happen, it was going to be bad. I'd never witnessed vampires fighting each other, but after seeing my vampire friends, François and Angelique, protecting me and fighting bad guys, I suspected that this time it could be ten times more gruesome.

After a while, Tudor cleared his throat. "Cat, how are you doing?"

"I'm all right. You?"

"Bewildered. I'm still trying to process what happened. I feel as if it were a terrible nightmare."

"I'm so sorry that I got you into this," I apologized again.

"It's all right. I hope we'll be able to spend time together in a more comfortable location."

"You can count on that." The thought of being with Tudor, spending leisurely time in his arms, gave me new vigor.

The silence fell on us again. In the dark, I couldn't tell how fast or slow time was passing, and I wondered how long we'd be in there. I heard Tudor stretching out on the bottom of the next cage. I decided to do the same, and I fell asleep.

I was awakened by the noise of a metallic ping coming down the stairs. It sounded as if a metal ball were bouncing down the stone steps. The sound stopped when the ball or whatever it was plopped into the ashes. I perked up my ears. Now I heard a buzzing sound. What could that be?

A bright light appeared at the top of the stairs, and the buzzing intensified. It was a drone. Fakeula had sent a drone ahead to check on our status. Would he have a cow when he saw the ashes?

"Do you see that? It looks like a drone," said Tudor.

A quad-propeller drone with lights and most likely a camera came down below our cages and searched the crypt, turning 360 degrees. After that inspection, the drone rose up between our two cages, and the camera inspected us, one at a time. I held my hand up to shade my eyes from the light. I hoped we looked convincing, as if we had never left our cages.

The drone ascended to the ceiling, inspecting the crypt from high above, turning in a tight circle in the middle of the hanging ropes. Tudor snatched one of the nearby ropes and gave it a snap. The rope undulated and hit the drone. The gizmo tilted and flew away from the rope, but whoever was controlling it overcompensated, so that the drone slid back toward the rope that had hit it. Tudor swiveled the rope and hit it again, this time from behind, pushing the drone into the forest of ropes. Bad news. The drone bounced from rope to rope while descending, until it reached the end of one rope that got caught in one of its propellers. It began twisting itself around the rope, resembling a mad fly caught on a sticky tape, swirling around while climbing and twisting up the rope. Finally, it quit. Although the propellers stopped, the light stayed on, turning around and illuminating the room in wide circles. Tudor sat back down in his cage, sneering.

The vampire who had sent the drone in saw what he wanted to see. We were in our cages, but there was complete disaster around us, no zombies hanging from the ropes, no proto-vampires in their coffins. What would he do next? Send in the cavalry? I hoped he hadn't spotted Mundibuto. The show was about to begin.

A flickering light came down the stairs. A dark figure descended, holding a torch. It was Fakeula. He stopped midway and gaped at the landscape below. The light from the drone kept rotating, sending random light beams around the crypt. Fakeula stood immobile. He was alone.

"Nooo!" he shouted in anguish, seeing the decimation of his army.

My cage was closer to him. I was on my feet, holding on to the bars. "Let us out of here!" I screamed theatrically.

He raised his head slowly and looked at me with despair in his eyes. "What did you do with the army, bitch?" he hollered.

"What army, Fakeula?" I played dumb.

"What happened here?" he shouted at the top of his lungs.

"Well, remember the blue, luminescent cloud around the tower?"

He went rigid and kept his eyes locked on me.

I cleared my throat. "It came in here and pulverized everyone in here except us."

He threw his torch down the stairs, raised both his arms, and howled like a wolf. "I'm going to drink your blood until you're dead!" He was pointing to me with a shaky finger.

"I wonder what that cloud would do to you if I summoned it now?" I spoke boldly, knowing full well that the cloud was gone. "The proto-vampires exploded in flames," I added.

"You . . . you . . . bitch!" He was enraged, shaking his fist at me now. "Ilie, Nicolae—get them!"

The two vampires entered the crypt from the ceiling, and when they were above us, they slid down the chains and landed on our cages. They looked ready to tear us apart.

Nicolae was on my cage. His eyes were about to pop out with fury. If Mundibuto didn't intervene soon, this monster would wring my neck. I backed away in the cage, terrified by him. I couldn't think of any defense to invoke from my Strigoi.

Chapter 26

"Stop!" shouted Fakeula.

Everyone stopped to look at him. A medieval axe was at his throat, and Mundibuto was holding him off the floor by his sleek hair. It turned out that Fakeula was afraid for his life.

"You escaped?" Ilie was incredulous to see Mundibuto. He jumped down onto the floor. Puffs of dust exploded around his feet.

"Surprise, surprise," tittered Mundibuto.

Nicolae followed Ilie down, making more dust. "This time we'll make sure you're dead before we dump you in a hole."

"I will enjoy killing you, too, Nicolae. You miserable, yellow coward!" boomed Mundibuto.

"Get Cat!" Fakeula squealed but stopped short of saying more when the axe blade pressed deeper on his throat.

"What for? We are three and he's only one," sneered Nicolae.

Technically, it looked to me as if there were only two against Mundibuto. Fakeula had his neck on an axe blade. I realized then how much I loathed Fakeula. He took on the image of my great-grandfather, and he was going to drink my blood until I died? I think not. I may not be a vampire, but I had Strigoi and hopefully I knew how to use them this time. Fakeula was mine to kill, or so I desired.

I turned and made eye contact with Tudor. "Whatever you do, do not come out of the cage."

"What do you intend to do?" Tudor asked nervously.

"You may want to close your eyes," I told him. He looked terrified but kept his eyes open.

Down below Nicolae and Ilie exchanged quick glances.

"I'll cut his head off if you get near Cat's cage," boomed Mundibuto.

Nicolae looked up at me, weighing his alternatives: let Fakeula die and get me, or try to get out alive from this standoff. I saw it in his eyes. He made his decision.

Just as quickly, I lowered my hands, palms down, and thought, *Lower my cage.*

Nicolae, followed by Ilie, jumped toward my cage but they missed it, because my cage was on the ground as quickly as they had jumped. Both of them hung on the opposite wall like two spiders.

I rolled out of my cage and stood up.

"Cat, what are you doing?" Mundibuto shouted, afraid for my safety.

Just as he said that, Fakeula squirmed, pulled himself away from Mundibuto's axe, and ran to get me. Mundibuto threw the axe at Fakeula, but Fakeula managed to avoid the blade. He was coming at me at an incredible speed, fingers ready to grab me by the throat. I raised my arms up high and pirouetted like a skater, helped by my Strigoi. Fakeula grabbed air, but in the blink of an eye, he flipped over to catch me again. I continued swirling like a top. He couldn't get his hands on me.

"Surprised?" I smiled mischievously at Fakeula.

He was at a loss. "How can you . . .?"

Little did he know about being able to use my Strigoi for defense. I gave him a mean smile.

"Mundibuto, you dispatch the two traitors who killed my great-granduncle Vlad the Impaler, and I'll take care of this bastard."

No sooner had I finished saying that when Nicolae and Ilie sprang toward me. I quickly moved out of the way, and they landed in a heap on the ground. They didn't have a chance to do anything else because Mundibuto was on them, swinging his other axe. Surprisingly, Fakeula did not come after me but joined the other two in trying to overcome Mundibuto. Although there were three of them and they had surrounded Mundibuto, he had the advantage of the axe, which the others darted around quickly to avoid. The other axe lay in the ashes. I lifted it, and with all my strength, I threw it to Mundibuto.

Instead, Nicolae jumped up and caught it. Mundibuto swung his axe to crack Nicolae's skull, but Ilie jumped on his back and Fakeula tackled his legs. Ilie had Mundibuto in a chokehold, while Fakeula was trying to topple him. Nicolae lifted his axe and brought it down on Mundibuto's head. Mundibuto twisted quickly to avoid the blow, and at the same time he lifted the axe up and behind him to hit Ilie's head. Ilie received a blow from Nicolae's axe, by mistake, which shaved off the hair on one side of his head. Mundibuto's axe shaved off the other side. Cracking a vampire's head open required a straight blade hit; otherwise, the axe would only graze the skull. Ilie was stunned, but he held on with his new Mohawk haircut. Mundibuto took hold of Nicolae's axe just below the blade. He quickly swung the axe at Nicolae, but Nicolae caught his axe in the same fashion.

Mundibuto needed help. Both of his massive hands held on to the axes just like Nicolae, while trying to overcome each other. Fakeula held his legs from behind, and Ilie was on his back, holding him in a chokehold. I jumped high and came down with both my feet on Fakeula's back. It was not a moment too soon. Although it felt as if I had landed on a stone statue, hardly hurting Fakeula, he released Mundibuto and turned back in a blur to catch me. I couldn't overcome Fakeula and jumped to get away.

Released from Fakeula's shackles, Mundibuto spun around and Nicolae became airborne. Mundibuto smashed Nicolae into the nearby wall with such force that dust blew out of the mortar joints. Mundibuto didn't give him a chance to recover and smashed him with his massive chest. I saw Nicolae's tongue come out and his eyes bulge. He slid down the wall, and he let the axes go. Unfortunately, Mundibuto lost his grip on Nicolae's axe, and it slid away. Mundibuto swung his axe at Nicolae, but a moment before the blade would make contact with his neck, Nicolae moved out of the way. The axe hit the stonewall, creating a shower of sparks. Nicolae ran and picked up the lost axe.

Fakeula lunged and latched his hands onto my ankles. Shit! Two times shit! He pulled me down, and it knocked the wind out of me.

Chapter 27

I couldn't fight a vampire, only escape from him. Fakeula stood up, holding me upside down by my ankles, as if I were a fish. I concentrated and, with the help of my Strigoi, I swung up with my back straight. Strong as he was, Fakeula couldn't oppose the momentum of my swing, and he fell on his back, with me on my feet straddling him. I didn't give him a chance to recover. I ordered my Strigoi to do lateral flips with me. We landed hard several times in a cloud of dust. While I continued landing on my feet, Fakeula always landed on his back, but he wouldn't let me go. I flipped backward, and Fakeula's head smashed into the wall behind us. He unclenched his hands but landed on top of me, dazed. The ashes cushioned my fall slightly. I pushed him away and rolled sideways, quickly distancing myself from him. I could not afford to let him or the others get hold of me again.

But that still didn't solve the problem at hand: disposing of them. I circled Fakeula, who was back on his feet, unsure of how to tackle me. Some distance away, Mundibuto was axe battling with Nicolae, while every so often he smashed backward against the wall to get rid of Ilie, who was still on his back.

Mundibuto swung his axe but missed. Nicolae brought his axe down hard on him. Mundibuto could not block the blow, so instead he turned his back, using Ilie like a shield. The axe sliced deeply into Ilie's back. Blue blood oozed thickly around the blade. Nicolae cried out in alarm and pulled the axe out. Ilie lost his hold on Mundibuto and fell off him.

Without hesitation, Mundibuto swung the axe at Nicolae and hit him on the upper right side of his chest. Nicolae grabbed the axe stuck in him and swung his axe at Mundibuto's axe arm, slicing the forearm to the bone, and Mundibuto released his axe. That was the best Nicolae could have hoped for—he couldn't attack any longer. He rested, with his back to the nearest wall, and wrenched the axe slowly from his chest to minimize the blood loss. Mundibuto clasped his left hand on his right forearm to seal the wound. His wound would close in seconds, without much blood lost, but the muscle had to heal before he could attack again. Ilie stumbled back to his feet, his wound probably closed by now, but one of his lungs was punctured, just like Nicolae.

The only vampire who was not cut was Fakeula. He, too, watched with dismay as his cohorts had to rest and heal. His head took a bashing, but he was in the best condition of all. Surprisingly, he did not attack Mundibuto or me.

"Cat, bottom of the stairs!" Mundibuto shouted at me.

There was something at the base of the stairway that he wanted me to find. Fakeula understood the same thing and jumped at me. I spun out of his way and ran to the stairway. Mundibuto came to my help: He jumped high and landed with his feet on Fakeula's back, knocking him down. Fakeula rolled and got back up. Mundibuto, still holding his arm, was between him and me.

An Uzi was near the wall of the stairway. I picked it up. The darn thing was heavy, but I held it up the best I could. I knew that it must have a safety. Was it on? Better question, where was it? I looked but couldn't find it. Only once in my life had I fired a weapon; it was a .38 revolver, and it had a nasty kick. I grasped the firearm firmly and pointed it at Fakeula.

Mundibuto was blocking the other vampires from my aim. Nicolae and Ilie didn't waste any more time in healing and retrieved the axes, advancing to attack. Mundibuto faced them, but Fakeula seized him from behind in a bear hug. Mundibuto has holding his right forearm and had only his legs with which to defend himself. I lifted the Uzi over their heads and squeezed the trigger. It fired. The recoil jerked the barrel up. I closed my eyes and dropped the gun.

The vampires stopped and stared at me. Running and evading them had been easy, compared to handling the Uzi. Mundibuto took advantage of the millisecond delay in fighting, and he bent down, flipped Fakeula over his head, and freed himself. Ilie and Nicolae swung their axes at Mundibuto. Fakeula jumped to his feet and instead of joining the fight, he sprinted toward me again. He wanted the gun.

I scrambled to get it off the ground. It was half buried in the ashes. I grabbed it by the barrel, but it was hot and I dropped it again. Fakeula rammed me with his shoulder, and I flew into the air. I had the state of mind to think *soft landing*. The Strigoi landed me gently on my feet. A few yards away, Fakeula bent down to retrieve the gun.

"Shoot him, Tudor!" Mundibuto shouted, while spinning, punching and jumping at his opponents.

What? Tudor was still up in his cage, and until now everyone had ignored him. He was holding an Uzi aimed at Fakeula. Suddenly, bullets peppered Fakeula's body. He staggered backward from the impact and dropped the gun.

With axes high, Nicolae and Ilie came flying down on Mundibuto to chop him in half. Mundibuto must have noticed my expression of horror and jumped up onto the ceiling. His arm seemed to have healed, because he was hanging on all fours.

The axe-wielding vampires looked up at him. They couldn't jump up after him—they needed all their limbs for that, and they didn't want to give up their axes. Fakeula was dazed from the bullets that had hit him, and he was sitting down as if to catch his breath. With the other two vampires distracted, I sprinted to where the Uzi was near Fakeula and found it. It was mine. I aimed the barrel at Fakeula's shocked face.

"Good night, bitch!" I pushed the barrel into Fakeula's mouth and squeezed the trigger. I held it tight so as not to lose control of it, and I emptied the magazine through his mouth. The back of his head blew away, leaving behind a blue hole. He collapsed. Incredibly, his skull was already folding in on itself to close the wound and preserve the remaining brain.

"Kill her!" shouted Nicolae, and both vampires ran toward me with their axes held high.

Tudor shot them from above, but he couldn't stop them. I had to get out of the way, so I dropped the empty gun. *Lift me up to the cage*, I commanded, and I leaped up on top of Tudor's cage. Mundibuto dropped down to the ground to fight the remaining two vampires, but they jumped up on top of the cage to finish me off. From underneath, Tudor discharged his entire magazine at them. Nicolae lost his balance, dropped his axe, and fell off. Ilie was hit, too, but stayed on his feet and raised the axe to kill me. His axe didn't come down, though. Mundibuto had jumped up, grabbed the axe from behind, and pulled Ilie off the cage. The two of them struck the ground in an explosion of dust.

"Are you OK?" I asked Tudor.

"Are you OK?" he asked me from the cage.

"I've got to go!" I jumped to the ground and landed gently.

Nicolae was writhing on the floor; the bullets must have hit him somewhere vulnerable. Mundibuto and Ilie were fighting over the axe, both of them holding it by the handle. Nicolae's axe lay nearby. Fakeula was flat on his back; with the back of his skull blown away, he wasn't going anywhere.

Nicolae was having convulsions and shaking, lying on his back. He was conscious enough to see me retrieve the axe, raise it over my head, and stand over him. His eyes were wide with fear. I held up the axe and cried, "This is for Vlad the Impaler!"

Whack! His head rolled away. His decapitated body kept convulsing and jerking. I pushed at his head with the axe. Unbelievably, he was conscious.

He stared at me with murderous eyes, but there was nothing he could do.

"I'm going to put your head in a jar of honey, like you did to Vlad." It felt good to say that, although I wasn't going to do any such thing. He closed his eyes and died.

Above me I heard Tudor retching. Who wouldn't vomit, even a doctor, seeing a decapitation? Fortunately for me and thanks to Mundibuto's voodoo elixir that he had given me in the past, death and dismemberment did not affect me.

Mundibuto wrestled the axe from Ilie, threw him against the wall, and, with a swift blow, he embedded the axe in Ilie's heart. Ilie slid down onto his butt, propped against the wall.

Ilie wasn't dead, though; his lips were moving. Mundibuto bent down and listened. "We will pay for this? Is that what you're saying? You'll be avenged?" Mundibuto said.

Ilie nodded.

"And who will avenge you?"

Ilie gurgled, "The Queen."

"I'm glad you mentioned her. Was this her army?" Mundibuto motioned with the axe at the hall.

"Yes. You're as good as dead," he whispered.

"The only hope you have is to meet her in hell." Mundibuto swung the axe and beheaded Ilie. His Mohawk shaved head bounced once and ended right side up in the ashes, looking as if he were buried up to his neck in them.

Chapter 28

Mundibuto walked slowly to Fakeula and chopped his head off. "Better to be sure that none of them ever live again." The surest way to kill a vampire was to behead him. Sure, Fakeula had half his brain blown away, but he might recover even with less gray matter and live on.

The vampires were dead. I dropped the axe and wiped my face with my hands. From that moment on, I was a vampire slayer as well. Of course, thanks to my Strigoi—without them to help me get away from the vampires, I would have been dead.

Mundibuto came to me with his arms open, and we hugged for a long while.

"Cat, I've never seen any human kill a vampire before."

"It had to be done." I held my head against his chest.

"A mighty weapon you have in your Strigoi."

I nodded. "I'm alive because of them."

"We're alive because of them." He was shaking his head in disappointment. "I thought I could handle the three of them, but without your help, your Strigoi, and Tudor, I could have been the one without a head."

"How's your arm?" I asked with concern.

"It's OK now." Mundibuto looked up at Tudor. "Do you want to come down?"

"Catch me," said Tudor. "My legs are shaking badly."

Mundibuto caught him easily in his arms and put him down. I ran to Tudor and embraced him with all my heart. His whole body was trembling. I caressed his face to calm him down.

Mundibuto returned with a bottle of *palinca*. "This may calm your nerves." He offered it to Tudor, who lifted the bottle in salute and took a long swig. Tudor exhaled to overcome the liquor's burn. He offered it to me, but I demurred. One-hundred-proof liquor was not my cup of tea. I was good.

"How did you get the Uzi?" I asked Tudor.

"Mundibuto gave it to me before he lifted me up in the cage."

I looked thankfully to Mundibuto, who smiled, satisfied that his plan B and C had paid off.

"And you knew how to fire it."

"I was in the reserves. I've handled guns before." Tudor smiled at me and took another drink. Then he passed Mundibuto the bottle.

After taking a long drink, Mundibuto said, "Here is what I need to do—I have to dispose of the bodies and the spilled blood."

"Where are you going to take them?"

"A secret place." He winked at me. I understood. He would dump the bodies and the spilled blood into the shaft he was thrown in earlier.

"Hopefully, they will all decay before anyone finds them," I said.

"I got just the thing." He showed me a yellow metallic can with the radioactive symbol on it. "Vampire decaying powder."

I raised my eyebrows but didn't ask for an explanation, considering that Tudor was present. "Do you need any help?" I asked him.

Mundibuto shook his head.

"Do you feel better, Tudor?" I asked.

"Yes, I do. Now," he said, swaying. The *palinca* had done its job.

"So this was Queen Eleonore von Schwarzenberg's army." I looked at the ashes left from her mighty army of zombies and proto-vampires. "She'll be pissed off."

"That's why, after this, I'll visit her so we can come to an understanding," said Mundibuto.

"What understanding?"

"I need to understand why she created her army. And she needs to understand that I'll kill her if she does it again." We looked at each other and smiled. All would be well, I was sure.

"Let's get out of here." I gave Mundibuto a peck on the cheek, took Tudor by the hand, and headed for the stairway. But then I looked down at Fakeula's body. "Our stuff." I kneeled down and emptied Fakeula's pockets. Our wallets, phones, keys, and flashlights were in there. I even found my backpack bag in a corner. "Now we can go," I told Tudor.

Chapter 29

It was past midnight, and the moon was one night past full. The cemetery was quiet. A while back, I would have been frightened to walk at night in a cemetery, even holding Tudor's hand, but not anymore. It was peaceful to be among the crosses under the bright moon.

Back in town, I gave Tudor a long kiss. "Thank you for saving my life."

"Saving your life?"

"If it hadn't been for your marksman shooting, we would not have made it."

"You were terrific yourself." He pulled me by the hand toward his hotel.

"Tudor, we need to split up."

"What do you mean?" He was worried.

"I mean, you need to go to your hotel and I'll go to mine. Dorin and Stanca have been looking for me since the night I spread the ashes from the tower."

"Oh, OK. Let me take you to your place."

"I'll go alone."

"Are you sure?" He looked around.

"Who would be the fool to touch me? I'll see you tomorrow morning." I gave him a longer kiss and took the street down through the Clock Tower to my inn.

The stair railing was patched up with fresh lumber. It felt as if I had been here a long time ago. I hoped they had left my bag in my room. I badly needed a soothing bath and clean clothes.

My room was intact, except for having been inspected by Dorin and Stanca, no doubt. I discarded my clothes and took a long bath. Afterward, it was good to be back in my cotton pajamas, lying in bed, staring at the ceiling. I had come here to spread Vlad's ashes. Instead, we killed the traitors who assisted in the murder of Vlad the Impaler and destroyed an army of monsters. Life was unpredictable.

The next morning, the hotel phone's ringing woke me up. "Hello."

"Cat, are you in? Are you OK? Are you safe?"

"Dorin? Good morning. Sure, I'm OK."

Stanca spoke this time. "We thought you were kidnapped, dear. We heard you calling for help the other night."

"Ohh, that." I needed to think of an explanation. "I'll explain everything over breakfast. Let me call Tudor to join us."

Dorin spoke, "Cat, there is a problem."

"What problem?"

"Dr. Tudor Lupu is under arrest."

"What?" I jumped up. "Why? What are the charges?"

"Kidnapping."

"Who did he kidnap?"

"Well . . . you."

"Oh, for crying out loud. He was with me all the time. Where is he?"

"At the police station."

I dressed in under a minute and ran out the door. Dorin, Stanca, and a policeman were waiting for me at the bottom of the stairs.

"Good morning," said the policeman.

"Where's Tudor? Let him go."

"All in good time, but where were you these past two days?"

"It's a long story. I'll tell you as we go to the police station to get Tudor out."

We got in the police car, and I babbled nonsense about Tudor being arrested. What story had Tudor divulged to them? It took only two minutes to arrive at the police station, not enough time to think up a good story.

I ran in and asked, "Where is Dr. Lupu?"

They took me to a room with a barred window, a desk, and two chairs. Tudor sat in one of the chairs, sleeping.

I shook him. "Tudor, wake up. I came to get you out."

He opened his eyes and smiled. "Cat, you're here. Tell these cops that I was with you all the time." He sounded and looked drunk.

"Well?" said the policeman, opening his hands as if inviting me to spill the beans. "What happened? Where were you? We searched for you all over."

"Thank you. It's nice to know that the Romanian police are on their toes to protect tourists. However, nothing extraordinary happened."

Dorin, Stanca, and the policeman raised their eyebrows in disbelief.

"OK." I sighed—I was going to have to wing it. "If you want to know, I'll tell you. I hope I didn't break any laws. As you know, I'm an American, and we Americans are crazy about Dracula." I raised my hands in the air, feigning excitement.

"Dracula?" exclaimed the policeman.

"This is the land of Dracula, isn't it?"

He nodded.

"I asked Dr. Tudor to escort me in search of Dracula. That's all."

"What about your call for help from the tower?" Stanca asked.

"Oh, that. Well, the best time to search for Dracula, I thought, was at night, and we were wandering through town when we found the tower's door open. Dr. Tudor did not want to go inside, but I persuaded him to go to the top with me. Foolish me—when I saw people searching for me, I jokingly yelled for help."

"Really? How come we didn't find you at the top of the tower?" Dorin asked.

"I realized that I had done a stupid thing, so we evaded you not to get into trouble."

They looked unconvinced.

"Oh, yeah. Now I remember," said Tudor, nodding.

"And then what happened afterward?" the policeman asked.

"We ran to the cemetery. What better place to explore for Dracula, don't you think?"

"And what did you do there?"

"We roamed the cemetery until we found an opening to a crypt and went in." I made a dumb face.

"What crypt?" The policeman was suspicious.

"I have no idea. It was dark, and once we were in, we got lost."

"For two days you were underground? In some unknown crypt?"

"Yeah. Or catacombs. Whatever. Afterward, I realized it was a bad idea, but we couldn't find our way out. We didn't have food or water with us, just two little flashlights, and it was creepy down there. The worst part is, we didn't find Dracula."

They all exchanged bewildered looks as if thinking, *crazy American girl.*

"Why didn't you call from your mobile?" Dorin asked.

"Dead batteries."

The policeman cleared his throat. "Did you break the lock on Lakinger's mausoleum?"

I shrugged. "We panicked, trying to get out after such a long time, but I don't remember where we were. It was dark the whole time." I bit one of my thumbnails, affecting sincere innocence. "I'll be glad to pay for any damage and fines."

The policeman placed his hands on his hips. "If you were in a crypt, how come Dr. Lupu is drunk?"

"Well, he wasn't drunk last night when we parted company and returned to our hotels." I looked at Tudor, inviting him to explain.

Tudor hiccupped. "Well, Officer, what would you do after coming out of a crypt after almost two days? You'd drink, too."

The policeman's shoulders slumped. He was convinced he was dealing with idiots. "Very well, you may go. And we'll assess the damage. We expect to be paid in cash."

"Please let me know, and I'll be glad to pay," I said with relief.

Dorin and Stanca looked at me, as if they knew that what I'd said was far from the truth. But officially, they weren't cops and, without disclosing their true identity, could not interrogate us. We were gone for almost two days, and that was that.

"In that case, I thank you." I took Tudor's hand and pulled him after me. "Tudor, you need some breakfast."

We were sitting at an outdoor café enjoying the sunny day and a large breakfast.

"I've never heard anyone lie like you," Tudor said between bites of sausage. He had "sobered up" the moment we left the police station.

"Do you have nut houses in Transylvania?"

"Nut houses? You mean mental institutions? Sure we do."

"Which one do you think they'd have thrown us into if I had told them the truth?"

"The biggest one." He chuckled.

"And speaking of lying, you play a pretty good drunk." I raised an eyebrow.

"Keep your mouth shut if you don't want to get into trouble." He gave me a knowing smile.

"We play well together." I leaned over and kissed him.

He looked very pleased but resumed his breakfast.

"Now that the worst is over, how would you like to join me on a vacation?" I wiggled my eyebrows.

"After what we've been through, you still want to see Transylvania?"

"Sure, my roots are here. I'd like to know the land and spend some quality time with you."

"But what about them?" He motioned with his head in the direction where Dorin and Stanca might be spying on us.

"I'll pay them in full and dismiss them. I have a better companion now." I took a sip of my coffee like a proper lady. I kissed him again and added, "and guide and lover."

Tudor blushed. "You make me feel like a teenager on prom night. I'd be ecstatic to show you around." Tudor winked at me and leaned over, and we kissed again. "What do you think our friends Dorin and Stanca are thinking as they watch us kissing?"

"Let the mystery keep them up at night."

And we had a wonderful time in beautiful Transylvania.

The End

Other Books by Mit Sandru

Thank you for reading my book. If you enjoyed it and would like to help other readers with your comments please write a review on Amazon. And of course I much appreciate your review as well **Amazon book** link.

For more information about my books please visit **sandru.com**

Or visit me at my website: sandru.com and subscribe to my mailing list.

(your e-mail will not be sold or used for spam)

Vampire Thriller & Romance

Vampire (Vlad V Series), by Mit Sandru, a Vampire Romance.

Vampire (Vlad V, Book 1) by Mit Sandru.

Meeting a vampire isn't something that happens every night, even on the New York City subways. Even in her wildest dreams Cat never expected to meet a vampire or survive an encounter with one. Instead, she becomes his confidant. Why is she so lucky?

R.I.P., The Death of a Vampire (Vlad V, Book 2) by Mit Sandru.

The US intelligence agencies have a massive database, including pictures that can identify any person in the US and abroad. A search has found a photograph of Vlad V Draculesti, a man living in present-day Manhattan, dating from 1851. How can that be? Why does Vlad look the same in the 21st century as he did in the 19th? Who is this man who has lived such a long life?

Homeland Security Federal Agent John Miller discovers that Vlad V Draculesti is a vampire, and he blackmails Vlad for billions of dollars, threatening to divulge that information to the authorities or to the evil Dr. Hellinherr, who is trying to create a super-race of people through the use of vampire blood.

But Vlad V, because of a mishap, is now dying of old age, and all he wants is to die in peace. Cat Sanders, his great-granddaughter, and his three vampire friends— François, Angelique, and Mundibuto—come to his rescue. They foil the intelligence agencies' plans to discover the real identity of Vlad V Draculesti, and they eliminate the corrupt federal agent's threat. Never underestimate a vampire, his cunning great-granddaughter and his vampire friends.

Vampire Slayers (Vlad V, Book 3) by Mit Sandru.
Vlad V the vampire warned Cat that when you're rich,
the stakes are much higher, and that she might have to
do appalling things to survive. Cat thought she'd have to
deal with unscrupulous lawyers, greedy financiers and
bankers, Wall Street shysters, corrupt politicians,
devious conmen, and depraved socialites. Instead, an old
nemesis allied with a vampire-slayer drug cult came out
of the dark, demanding extortion money or she would be
killed. Capturing a vampire—Vlad V perhaps—would be
an added bonus for the cult. Blue vampire blood could
provide perpetual life and additional riches.
Unfortunately, the villains don't know who or what they
are dealing with. Never upset the great-granddaughter
of Vlad V and Angelique, her vampire friend, if you want
to stay healthy and alive.

Vampires of Transylvania (Vlad V, Book 4)

Cat has a simple task ahead of her: spread Vlad V Draculesti's ashes in Transylvania at midnight during a full moon. But it won't be that simple. She comes across Vlad V and Vlad the Impaler's old enemies and a sinister plot concocted by the Queen of Vampires. By discovering the queen's plot, Cat finds herself in mortal danger.

Luckily, the African vampire Mundibuto and a new friend, Dr. Tudor Lupu, come to her aid. She has to use all the tricks she can muster to stay alive and take revenge on Vlad the Impaler's assassins.

Soon to be published:

The Queen of Vampires (Vlad V Book 5), by Mit Sandru

Other Books:

The Pregnant Pope (TIO Series), by Mit Sandru.

In the year of Satan, 2066, the structure of the physical world is cracking, and inexplicable paranormal forces are interfering with humanity. The Trinity Investigation Organization, or TIO—a paranormal detective society— is the last protection against the demons, evil spirits, fanatical criminals, and sadists who are trying to destroy the world.

The 92-year-old Pope is pregnant. Although he hasn't undergone any medical procedures, he carries a human fetus in his abdomen. Is this a case of self-cloning, or is it a mutation? Is this an immaculate conception, or is it Satan's work?

Claire, Travis, and Prescott, the members of the Capuchin Trinity Team of TIO, are tasked with uncovering the truth about this unusual case and resolving the mystery of whether the Pope is carrying the new Messiah or the Antichrist, and who did it. Their job is to go beyond the physical world into the mind and the spiritual realm, discover a thousand-year-old connection, perform an exorcism, and fight the devil Zepar, while evading the villains who keep trying to assassinate them.

Folding Reality, by Mit Sandru, a Paranormal, Time Travel Adventure.

Experiencing a new reality is just a paper-fold away for Mike the insurance salesman. But those realities are not by his choice and he ends up being crucified, or gassed at Auschwitz, or marooned in space in a Russian capsule.

Arboregal, the Lorn Tree, by D.G. Sandru, a Teen Fantasy and Science Fiction adventure.

Four young Americans are magically transported to a world where monsters roam the land, magnificent trees support all life, and an evil spirit hunts one of them to fulfill a deadly prophecy.

Escape from Communism, by Dumitru Sandru, a True Story and Commentary.

Life under communism is cruel and inhumane. Communist countries have a "Berlin Wall" around them, and the whole country is a giant concentration camp. I risked my life to escape from hell and reach freedom.

T-Shirts and other stuff:

Sandru's Shop or Sandru's Products

Visit my e-Gallery at:
http://dumitru-sandru.artistwebsites.com/
http://www.artistrising.com/galleries/Sandru

About Dumitru "Mit" Sandru
Dumitru "D.G." "Mit" Sandru was born in the greater area of Transylvania in the last century. He is an artist, composer, and author. He paints in the classical, surreal, and modern styles, and most of the music Dumitru composes is of the New Age flavor. As an author, he prefers to write Science-Fiction, Paranormal, and Teen/Children Fantasy & Sci-Fi novels.
Dumitru resides in California with his wife. They have one daughter and two grandsons.
Visit him at **sandru.com**